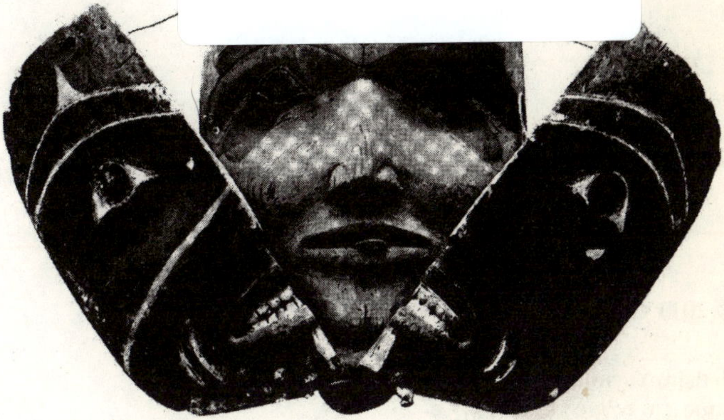

Double dance mask of the Haida.
Queen Charlotte Islands, Canada.

İletişim Yayınları 1678
ISBN-13: 978-975-05-0962-9

Reprinted 2011, 2012, 2018, 2022, 2023 / İstanbul

EDITOR Kıvanç Koçak
COVER DESIGN Hakkı Mısırlıoğlu
COVER Suat Aysu
COVER PAINTING Mehmet Nazım
LAYOUT Hüsnü Abbas
PRESSING Ayhan Matbaası · CERTIFICATE NO. 44871
Mahmutbey Mahallesi, 2622. Sokak, No: 6/31 Bağcılar 34218 İstanbul
Tel: 212.445 32 38 • Faks: 212.445 05 63
BINDER Güven Mücellit · CERTIFICATE NO. 45003
Mahmutbey Mahallesi, Devekaldırımı Caddesi, Gelincik Sokak,
Güven İş Merkezi, No: 6, Bağcılar, İstanbul, Tel: 212.445 00 04

İletişim Yayınları · CERTIFICATE NO. 40387
Cumhuriyet Caddesi, No. 36, Daire 3, Seyhan Apartmanı,
Harbiye Mahallesi, Elmadağ, Şişli 34367 İstanbul
Tel: 212.516 22 60-61-62 • Faks: 212.516 12 58
e-mail: iletisim@iletisim.com.tr • web: www.iletisim.com.tr

GÜNDÜZ Y. H. VASSAF

Prisoners of Ourselves

Totalitarianism in Everyday Life

iletişim

GÜNDÜZ Y. H. VASSAF, writer and psychologist, was educated in United States and Turkey. Having first worked as a clinical psychologist, he taught at Boğaziçi University, but resigned from teaching after the Turkish military coup of 1980 in protest against the law abrogating academic autonomy and freedom. Before turning to writing, he was a Research Fellow at the Institute of Higher Studies in Vienna, and subsequently Guest Professor in Germany at the Universities of Kassel, Marburg and Bremen. He has been on the Board of Directors of the International Council of Psychologists, was Regional Coordinator for Europe and the Middle East for the American Psychological Association Division of Community Psychology, a founding member of the Committee for Peace of the International Union of Psychological Science, and the founding member and head of the Istanbul group of Amnesty International.

Vassaf's books, published in Turkish and translated into several languages, focus on the psychology of everyday life, with an overreaching theme of the quest for individual freedom. His essays combine daily life with poetry, politics, anecdotes and jokes, sometimes provocative, always questioning issues such as personal and community identity; his collections of short stories take a penetrating, satirical look at the modern world, combining social comment with a sense of the absurd. A recurrent theme has been transitions between countries and cultures over time. Recently he has offered a radical re-evaluation of the nature and role of history in an age of electronic media, censorship and the manipulation of information. A leading figure in Turkish intellectual life, Vassaf has also had a weekly cultural column in the newspaper *Radikal* from its founding in 2007 until the papers last issue in 2016. In 2010-2011 he co-hosted a TV talk show covering a wide spectrum of intellectual debates. A biography of his life and work, based on a series of interviews with him was published in 2011.

Books by Gündüz Vassaf:
- *Zekâ ve Zekâ Testleri Nedir? Ne Değildir?* (Intelligence and Intelligence Tests) (1977)
- *Daha Sesimizi Duyurmadık* (We Have Yet To Be Heard: Turkish Workers' Children in Europe) (1983, 2002)
- *Cehenneme Övgü* (Prisoners of Ourselves-Totalitarianism in Everyday Life) (1992)
- *Cennetin Dibi* (Depths of Heaven) (1996)
- Annem Belkıs (My Mother Belkıs) (2000)
- *40 Yıl Önce 40 Yıl Sonra-Amerika Rusya* (2006) / *Gençliğimin Kayıp Yılları* (2022) (40 Years On: America and Russia) (2006)
- *Tarihi Yargılıyorum* (Judging History Judging Us) (2007)
- *Türkiye Sen Kimsin?* (Turkey Who Are You?) (2008)
- *Leventnâme* (The Levant Chronicles) (2009)
- *Kimliğimi Kaybettim Hükümsüzdür* (I Have No Flag, Religion or Gender) (2010)
- *Mostari: Bir Köprü Bekçisinin Günlüğü* (Mostari: The Diary of a Bridge Keeper) (2013)
- *Medeniyet, Kültür, Sanat* (Civilization, Culture and Art) (2014)
- *İstanbul'da Kedi* (The Cats of Istanbul) (2014)
- *Boğaziçi'nde Balık* (The Bosphorus Fish Tales) (2015)
- *Nazım* (Nazim) (2015)
- *Ne Yapabilirim?-Geleceğe Kartpostallar* (What Can I Do? Postcards to the Future) (2016)
- *Yol Arkadaşım: Havaalanı Yazıları*, (Stories from Airport) (2017)
- *Sınırsız* (Unrestricted) (2018)
- *Ressamın İsyanı* (The Painter's Rebellion) (2023)

ABOUT MYSELF

I was little. One day adults would not believe in something I experienced and I realized that my mother could be wrong. I couldn't hold myself back. I had a laughing fit.

At nine, I became afraid of others. While my mother and I were secretly watching from a hole in the shutters, a group of fifty to sixty people were on the verge of attacking our house. Earlier in the day our teacher had taught us a nationalist slogan which I had written in chalk on our car in the front garden. They noticed it. The pogrom in the city continued throughout the night.

When a few months after going to boarding school I received news that my cat (Tarzan) had died, I knew that one could die from loneliness and lack of love.

The head of the psychology department said that the language in my thesis had to be "purified." I did not object. This was my initiation into self-censorship. I now have a thesis that I can't understand.

I was working as an intern in the psychiatry clinic of the university hospital when a mother turned in her son with the hash she had found in his pockets. When the head of the unit, our professor, passed the hash around at a party in his home that night, I had become a colleague.

Just after the military coup, in order to stay at the university and comply with the junta, some academics shaved their beards. Some censored their past. Those who would not, resigned. I was one of them. I miss the students.

Once, I used influence so that our son could become a citizen. The consulate had refused, saying I was not married. A bastard cannot be given citizenship they said. Then in the same breath they objected to my family name, saying that it was against the law because it was of foreign origin. "How did you get such a name?" the consul demanded. I pointed to the giant portrait of the country's founding president. "He's a relative of my father. Must have been his doing," I said. Our son became a citizen.

Some years ago, after giving it much thought, I came to the conclusion that being a fireman was the least harmful of all professions. "Not so," a friend said, "In France firefighters secretly set fires to become heroes."

In recent years I have kept mostly to myself. From time to time, I cannot stop myself from writing. Had they asked me what should be done with the prison that just shut down, I would have said, make a museum with only mirrors inside.

TABLE OF CONTENTS

Introduction *13*

I. In Praise of Night *15*

II. Freedom in Hell *25*

III. Prisoners of Speech *33*

IV. No Longer Free: Madness in Modern Times *45*

V. Here We Eat, There We Sleep *65*

VI. Heroes Are Totalitarian *75*

VII. Informania *87*

VIII. What's Your Sex? *95*

IX. Freedom from Choice *109*

X. In Defense of Traitors *137*

XI. Death Forgetting *147*

XII. Beware of the Artist! *157*

XIII. Disagreement Forever *167*

XIV. Goals Against Life *175*

XV. Zap! You're Dead *189*

XVI. Homo Sapiens Blues *205*

XVII. Why Children? *229*

XVIII. This Magic Moment *239*

XIX. The Totalitarianism of Love (As Practiced) *251*

XX. To Be Drunk! *269*

In memory of Giardano Bruno (1548-1600)
who rejected the Pope's heaven.

To Çalıkuşu 11 and its residents

The absurd thing is that some philosopher has already said something even absurder before.

Marcus Tullius Cicero (106 B.C. - 43 B.C.)

What reallly needs to be explained is not why the hungry steal or the exploited go on strike, but why most of the hungry don't steal and the exploited don't go on strike.

Wilhelm Reich

INTRODUCTION

This book is about freedom.

It's about freedom we avoid. About freedom that we fear to have in our everyday lives. Even with our simple daily acts we subject ourselves to a totalitarian order of our creation and subservience.

My first idea was to write a book about our accommodation of totalitarian regimes. Throughout history, millions across the world have experienced changes in regimes from a relatively democratic state to a totalitarian order.

In the end and over time, we acquiesce to these regimes. We internalize the new norms. The very few who don't, become martyrs, unknown patients in mental hospitals, forgotten prisoners of conscience.

I did not write a book about the above because I realized that also in "democratic" regimes we can become prisoners of ourselves.

The essays are observations about how we imprison ourselves in our daily lives.

None offer solutions as such.

Solutions can only lead to other forms of totalitarianism.

Critical thinking and doubt, on the other hand, promote freedom.

Like all others, our species will also become extinct.

Whether we go as prisoners or in freedom is up to us.

Marburg, 1988

IN PRAISE OF NIGHT

I

Bottle, Rene Magritte, 1945

I was afraid and looked upon the moon.
I cried and my words reached the gods.
God of the moon, Sin,
Protect me.
Gilgamesh

I.

At night the forces of order are asleep. The bureaucracy, the military, the schools, the police, that is all those who give order to our lives are all asleep, except for the night police patrolling the streets. Of all the people in the world the earliest to sleep are the soldiers. The most oppressive of all institutions, the military, go to bed the earliest. In fact, in all totalitarian institutions, that is in all institutions (for are not all institutions totalitarian?) one must always go to bed early —boarding schools, monasteries, jails, hospitals.... I know of no institution that upholds the right, the freedom of the person to go to bed at any time that he or she pleases. Even in marriage, an institution brought about by the free will of two persons and based on love (?), problems soon arise when both don't go to bed at the same time, when one goes to bed later, lives the night more. The institution always blames the one who stays up "late", not the one who goes to bed "early." In European feudal society all people in town were forced to blow out their lights at exactly the same time except during festivals. It is in the nature of the forces of order and oppression that there must always be a fixed time for sleeping. It is also in their nature that the fixed time is always early.

II.

Throughout history and in all cultures we have been made to associate darkness with the forces of evil. We have been taught to be afraid of the night people, the people of the night, the people at night. But the day and night person are one and the same. Except that, while the day brings out the conformity in us, the night brings out freedom. The forces of order have conditioned us to avoid the night, to avoid freedom.

The establishment, whether it is religion, family, or the state looks at people at night with fear. For it is mostly during the night that they cannot control their subjects. Nighttime people are looked upon as suspect. No one can be up to any good at that hour. The forces of establishment that reign during the day justify their existence and oppression through the enemies of the night, whom we never see but only hear of in vague, abstract terms.

The rulers too are always shown to us, always show themselves to us, as a part of the day. A President, a general or a bishop may be pictured in the beauty of nature with a shining sun behind them; but never against the background of the night.

III.

Daytime is a monotonous process that seems to be progress. The change of light from the morning brightness to the evening darkness suggests to us a sense of progress—a feeling that we are proceeding in a certain direction. We rarely stop to think of the artificial relativity of time. The change from lightness to darkness during the day, each and every day, keeps us going. But, throughout the day, whether it's ten in the morning or three in the afternoon, we are all slaves to the order of the day, to the forces of establishment. It is only the passage of time and the promise of liberation at night that keeps us going. Because, we know eventually that there will be night and that we will (as compared to the day) have the opportunity to do as we please.

Books are read at night. Film, theatre, and music performances are at night. We get drunk at night. Gamble at night.

The bare, naked body belongs to the night. Bodies touch each other, come together during the night. What is discussed clinically at university lectures during the day, what is socially discussed and implied at social gatherings during the evening, finally takes place in secret in the darkness of the night. Nakedness is with the night. Not with the daytime. (The opposite which is the natural state of being naked under the sun, can only universally take place with the end of oppression.)

We fall in love, declare our love for one another at night. Day time calls us to our senses, to our prison. During the day the forces of oppression work against the freedom of love. It is only at night that we fall in love once more and say "I love you". "I love yous" of the day refer to the night.

IV.

We accept being prisoners during the working day so much that the remaining hours are referred to as our "free" time. The opposite of free time is the day time when most of us are at work.

Wars usually begin at the break of dawn. The state kills, executes as the day breaks. Burials and cremations belong to the day. We try to survive during the day and live at night. It is during the day that we pay the electricity bill, get the car fixed, go shopping, see the doctor and either go to jobs that we don't like or look for jobs that we won't like but need.

During the day we are regimented and ordered in all our tasks. Even going to the toilet has its strict limitations and regulations. At the workplace, school, military etc., one cannot go as often and as long as one pleases. Not only can one not go when one wants, but the frequency and length of time might even be recorded. Also, if one wants to go outside of the institutionally sanctioned times, one must get permission. We are not even free to go to the toilet as we please during the day, because the day time does not belong to us. Whoever heard of a factory worker reading a newspaper in the toilet?

Relations of people during the day are ordered. In schools young people end up being in the same rooms with the same people year after year just because they are the same age. Eight year olds in room six, ten year olds in room fifteen... And even then there is a permanent order of seating. It is only with the end of the school day and the coming of the evening that one can choose with whom one wants to be. If you are a soldier you spend almost all day with those who are the closest to you in height. It is only in the evenings and at night that a five-foot-eight person can be with a six-foot-five friend.

V.

The rigidity of the social classes breaks down at night. Workers stroll in the streets of the bourgeoisie. The bourgeoisie go to restaurants in the worker's area. Whores, priests, students, soldiers, housewives, doctors and foreigners all stroll down the same street, looking, thinking, talking to each other and perhaps eventually even "making love". The world becomes alive at night with the free intermingling curious spirit of the people. What is avoided during the day becomes attractive at night. The "rational" person of the day steps back and a pursuit of the senses takes over.

Even the oppressors, in spite of the fact that their own freedom too is curtailed by the act of oppressing, have more freedom at night. The rulers of the establishment, generals and kings, presidents of companies and countries, "the rich and famous" live the night. When the totalitarian institutions are asleep, have been put to sleep, they have the freedom to be as they really are. Like parents who have put their children to bed, they now have the freedom to show their unmasked faces without ceremony or censorship.

VI.

By nighttime the rush of the day is no longer there. We are more or less settled. For a good ten hours the initiative will be with us. We begin by choosing and creating what we eat. Daytime food for many is institutional and standardized. At night, not only do we have more choice of what to eat but also how it should be prepared. We also don't have to rush through a meal. What is called "fast food" belongs to the forces of oppression that dominate the day. As fast food eaters we are part of the totalitarian mega-machine that rules us. At night, as preparers of our own food, we give our own order to space and time.

VII.

Daylight is a decoy. Light blinds us. It is at night that our eyes are wide open. All our other senses are also more attentive, for the forces of order have shut down their machines. At night we listen to silence, see into darkness, give free reign to our bodies and imagination. One is no longer the consumer of countless messages that try to imprison our senses during the day. The constant humming of the oppressive megamachine has stopped. Now, the source of energy is within. The night is the background for man's performance of the mind.

During the day it is the performance of light, colour, motion to which we attend. And what we attend to is designed by the forces of order. Green and red lights even regulate when we cross streets. We attend during the day. During the day we are attendants. At best, we are the observers of the magic of life in the intricate pattern of the butterfly.

VIII.

As night is the time for sleep, it is also the time for dreams. Languages, forms, modes of behaviour, perceptual paradigms that limit what we see, hear, smell and think, do not apply to the structure of the dream which has its own particular language and form. Colours, images, people, emotions, thoughts are free to mix and create uniquely. In fact, dreams are so free that they cannot be recounted—told through the rigid structures that rule the mind and body of the person during the day.

Those who cannot sleep, those who have insomnia, are also those who cannot face the unlimited freedom and truth that darkness brings. During the day they occupy themselves by attending. At night there is nothing more to attend. Only the distinct voice of life comes from within. Absurdity, absracted from the day, is no longer in hiding. The person is more consciously aware of the fact that he is living and also that there is death. The "meaning of life" is felt and questioned at night. Nobody talks about it over lunch. Life is a subject of the night.

October 15, 1986, Marburg

of ... endless message ... [illegible] the constant murmuring of the [illegible] [illegible] ... [illegible] [illegible] ... [illegible] ... [illegible] ... [illegible] ... [illegible] ... [illegible] ... [illegible]

VIII.

Complete the time for sleep ... who produce [illegible] languages ... [illegible] ... what we see, hear, smell and think, do not apply to [illegible] particular language and form. [illegible] images, [illegible] thoughts are free to [illegible] ... [illegible] through the [illegible] structures that [illegible] the mind and body of our [illegible].

Those who cannot sleep, those who have no [illegible] ... those who cannot bear the [illegible] ... [illegible] brings. During the day, they occupy [illegible] ... at night there is nothing [illegible]. Only the [illegible] comes from within. [illegible] ... [illegible] ... [illegible] ... [illegible] ... Nobody talks about [illegible] ... sleep of the nights.

FREEDOM IN HELL

II

The Devil, Autun Cathedral, France
XII Century

"The devil: Better to rule in Hell than to serve in Heaven"
John Milton

I.

It all came together when I was visiting the cathedral in Toledo. Richard Crosfield took me by the pews and said that I must have a look under the seats. Perhaps about sixty in all. They were folded up so that no one could see the bottom. Underneath were various depictions of hell. The artist(s) had given their fantasy and imagination free rein. There were all sorts of monsters and gargoyles in various settings. Above the seats were carved the saints. Above the saints, various biblical events. And, on top of everything else, the Virgin and the Holy Child. All that which was above the seats, one can see in churches and paintings throughout the world. Although the quality and the art of the master change, what is depicted is the same. Given the rule, hierarchy and orthodoxy of the church, the artist has little leeway in projecting his particular "world." His only opportunity to create is in hell. While he is restrained in making the holy figures and scenes, in hell, the more he lets himself go, the better.

It is not only the painter, the artist, but also we, the observers, who are fascinated by hell and not heaven. One need only think of Bosch's triptych at the Prado. The crowd that daily gathers before it, push and shove to gather before hell. Very few are interested in looking at the idle monotony in heaven. Some museum visitors give a passing glance at heaven and many do not look at all.

The first man, Adam, chose to sin rather than be in heaven. He chose the vicissitudes of life over idle monotony. Heaven has never been a very interesting place in our imagination. It has not, cannot capture our imagination. Dante's *Divine Comedy* is another example. In the Inferno and to a degree the Purgatory, the author's and our imagination run wild - there is the ultimate freedom in imagining. Dante's Heaven on the other hand is as dull a place as there can be. It's so dull that very few of those who have read it can even remember it.

The medieval artist commissioned by the church or its patrons was fortunate. Today's artist cannot so easily share or express his creativity for the totalitarianism of "modern times" has removed hell from our lives.

II.

Entrance to heaven depends on the judgement of others. It implies a hierarchical order of judges and the judged, of rulers and the ruled. On the other hand, nobody stands in the way between the person and hell. There is no one to please, no one to lie to (including oneself), no one to gain favours from, and no one to whom one offers sacrifices. An independent man will never get himself into a situation where he will allow himself be judged. It is also arrogant to judge. Hell is the abode of the free spirit.

III.

Today's governments, parties, ideologies all have a claim on establishing Heaven on Earth—a Heaven without Hell. All reminders of hell and death have been removed from the kingdoms in which we live. Cemeteries are in out of the way places instead of being near the village green or the town centre. State terror and executions are hidden from the public in contrast to how hell was discussed daily and torture openly practised when religion reigned. Today's hell on earth is censured. It is taboo.

The aim of life now is to become rich and live forever. The ideal death is that which comes suddenly. Concern for the afterlife has been replaced by a wish for immortality. Government statistics pride themselves on the increase in longevity. Everybody tries to look and act young. We are promised less work and more play-time. Robots will enable all of us to be slave owners, and there will always be more and more things to possess and more time to be idle, so we hope.

It is of course a heaven with no challenges, no initiatives, nothing to be curious about. There is no sense of that which is fleeting—the same thing day in day out.

Heaven is totalitarian because all governments prompt their citizens to live in their own particular image of heaven on earth. It is planned by experts and politicians. The picture of the ruler's heaven is so total, so unfailing in their eyes, that there is not even mention of hell. Hell, in the sense of an alternative, does not exist. At the most there are the so called alternatives between political parties.

IV.

Hell is the greatest challenge, the greatest threat to the ruling classes and parties. It suggests that they may be fallible, that they may be punished by forces greater than themselves.

The concept of hell suggests to the people a sense of eternal justice, in which their sufferings might be vindicated.

With hell abolished, the ruled no longer have the freedom to condemn their oppressors there. The only danger to the rulers are the assassins who kidnap and kill without any support from the people.

The rulers have used mass media to erase images of hell from our consciousness. In our condemned weakness we have no icons to turn to as the oppressed once did. While claiming heaven on earth, the totalitarianism in our century has abolished hell. It has abolished a sense of the other —other than life. Death and hell have been as far removed from our daily consciousness as possible. Life itself becomes a totalitarian concept if it cannot be considered in relation to death.

By abolishing hell, the rulers of today have reached the ultimate in totalitarian power. Until heaven on earth has its spiritual alternative in the reaffirmation of a hell and death, the totalitarian forces will grow stronger. Where there are no believers, mercenaries rule the day.

October 16, 1986, Marburg

PRISONERS OF SPEECH

III

Tower of Babel, Gustave Dore (1832-1883)

And thus they called it Babel; because that's where God mixed up all the tongues and scattered them across the earth.
Old Testament

I.

First there was the word. And the word was in the possession of God, the prophets, the priests. The word belonged to the powerful, to the ruler. In time more came to share the word. Trade, technology and the struggle against oppression facilitated the process. The printing press, the use of the vernacular, universal education and finally telecommunications put all in possession of the word. Everybody possessed the word and through it the world. In possessing the world, we reduced it from the WHOLE that it is, to bits and pieces that we have. And there we rule, worshipping our own words, idolizing ourselves.

II.

With words we fix a firm hold not only on objects but also on concepts and feelings. Words are a way in which we possess or try to possess, hold onto our experiences. It is perhaps the easiest way of storing and categorizing, committing experiences to memory. Once stored, we use them in much the same way as money in the bank. We use it when we need to. But just as the value of money changes overtime, so does the sense of the world associated with the word. As the context changes so does the content. The "same" word, in different contexts, is not quite the same. Nor is the time and space surrounding the word.

Words bring an order, a standardization to the world of objects and feelings. It is a standardization that exists neither in the material nor the spiritual world. Words are artificial constructs created by us to facilitate communication in order to promote a mutual, interdependent life. Words, by necessity, reduce things to common simplistic images, concepts and stereotypes, so that we may proceed with our self-appointed destiny of possessing, ordering and controlling nature and society.

III.

We use far too many words in fear that we won't understand each other. We fear that not using the spoken word implies not communicating, not wanting to communicate, impoliteness. We also speak far too much. Silence scares us. We cannot control silence. In silence there is the ultimate in freedom and randomness arising from the new impulses that we sense both from without and within. Using words imposes our order upon the (un)silent world. We feel secure. It is a sign of power emanating from our inclination to attend, to grasp that which is unknown, to codify into words for which there is no verbal cognitive map. By using words we possess things.

In possession we feel powerful, in control. That is the height of our folly—like the ostrich burying it's head in the sand. As substitutes, words prevent us from attending, from experiencing. The word makes us blind. The predominating activity of collapsing all our feelings and thoughts on a word, shuts, hampers a total understanding through the senses. We use the senses only as an auxiliary to the word, only to enhance the meaning of the word. Rarely is it the other way around, that the word is used to enhance the total experience of the senses.

We have become so accustomed to spoken language that we put the cart before the horse. Artificial categories have taken over the experiential. Our conceptions, which are more than the input of all the senses put together, have become equated with words.

Take love for instance, one of the most complex and varied experiences of our species. The words, "I love you," have become far more important than the look, the touch, the smell and the various sounds that express love. We try to possess love through the spoken word rather than share it through the mutual experience of the senses. As each love is different—different smells, ways of touching, ways of experiencing, different psychological roles—the words shared in each love would also be different— so one would think. Yet, no! The word is bigger than the world of experience. And the totalitarian possessing, "I love you" standardizes all love experiences. It quantifies love. We use words to bring arithmetic to love. "I have been in love three times!"

The possession and quantification of love by the use of the word goes against the experiential truth that love is heterogeneous, that it differs from person to person and experience to experience.

The word forces love into mutually exclusive categories. How many suffer, go mad, commit suicide, cause suffering in others, just because a state of love has to be affirmed, categorized by the words, "Who do you love, x or y?" It has to be one or the other. Mutually exclusive.

One can go on and on. "Which one of us do you love more, Daddy?" And Daddy, of course, because of the paradigm, the mental set ordered by the language, by the fact that the word reduces and possesses the experience rather than vice versa, feels compelled to avoid an answer. At the same time, perhaps secretly, perhaps unconsciously, he makes a choice of the one child he loves above the other, only because he is a prisoner of the word-paradigm. What if there were eight, twelve, fifteen different words for love? — less jealousy, less possession and a reinforcement of uniqueness rather than a reduction of standardization. No vertical hierarchy.

What if there were no words for love? Would love then cease to exist? Would it not be felt? Love was before the word.

IV.

From birth on, the more the child is trained in the use of spoken language, the more he wears a "straight-jacket" in terms of his relationship with life. The infinitely immense capability of the brain to differentiate, to see things both singly and in interchanging relations on the basis of their particular qualities and characteristics, becomes more limited when the child gradually confines himself to our words, to abstraction and to generalization. While there are infinite possibilities for various types of abstraction and generalization, the particular development of our civilization, and to a degree the course of our evolution, basically limits us to only one type of language-restricted abstraction.

Phylogeny recapitulates ontogeny. All the steps of evolution are repeated in the single individual's growth. It is a cultural accident that we now all learn to walk first and swim later. Actually, it is in our nature to swim first and learn to walk later. Had it been otherwise, had we been a primarily more balanced water/land civilization rather than being land-bound, our conscious sensitivity to the differentiation in the environment would have developed along different lines, and of course so too would our language. Our language is specific not to nature and the material world but rather to our particular way of relating to nature. Our capability of seeing and experiencing is far richer than the small, limited world in which language confines us.

Because of the spoken word, because of the exaggerated dominance of the spoken word, we consciously experience less. We see, hear, smell, touch, taste less. We bypass many experiences. We attend less to life and more to our simplification and particular abstraction.

Of the infinite variety that we could experience, the few that we actually do experience are immediately codified and standardized in words.

V.

A new danger limiting our sense of the world is that, in the so-called developed societies, in order to better control the masses and facilitate communication for the sake of efficient production and quick profit, not more but less words are being used—abbreviations, acronyms, shorter and more functional sentences, more functional words devoid of emotion and concept. Language is evolving into a simple form of computer speech. Spoken language is becoming more and more like a set of instructions that can be followed by human and machine alike.

Keeping up with the development in technology and the changes in the relationships of production we, of course, have new words. In that sense language is developing. But only in the manner that more profit is generated without an increase in production. It is not expanding our experiences with life and the universe. The cosmos, through the use of words, is now becoming the latest of our possessions. Words in this sense are like the flags of imperialism planted on newly captured lands. They very quickly define and order the new environment, which results in a standard mental set for many generations.

Despite new mental and physical contexts, and no matter what the world says, the word remains the same. The mental paradigm is always last to change.

VI.

Speechlessness leads to an expansion of the senses, silence to a heightened form of communication. For in silence we share a bonding that encompasses and goes beyond verbal exchanges. Silence is the gestalt of all that is sensed. The spoken word is an intrusion into silence, an intrusion into wholeness. It disturbs, differentiates, categorizes and finally reorders a minute part of our total experience. The mere uttering of a word is like throwing a stone into still water and not being able to see it as clearly as before because of the ripples. The word in that sense is the stone.

The spoken word is totalitarian. It orders. It possesses. It shuts others out. It creates a hierarchical relationship—one who speaks and one who attends. In all speech-exchanging relationships there is domination of one by the other. The spoken word, the act of speech is a very important, integral part of the order in which man dominates man. Words are necessary for people to be controlled and for people to control each other. There are hierarchical orders as to who can first break the silence, that person usually being the dominant one—"Do not speak until spoken to!" In the process of exchanged speech there is often competition to take over the speaking, to assume the dominant role. The words "I agree," "I understand," are used more to interrupt and take over the speech than to affirm communality. The power relationship in speech reflects differences between social class, sex and age. The act of speech reinforces the dominant-submissive order in all of these relationships. The exploited, the subjugated, in attempting equality, imitate the same relationship, try to possess the position of the oppressor by taking over their words, thereby, becoming the oppressor.

It is silence that breaks, astounds, surprises, makes one ill at ease. It is silence that is not ordered. It is silence that has both imminent and unknown possibilities. It is silence that perks our curiosity. It is silence that enriches our imagination. Experience, put into words, takes away from the experience.

Using fewer words does not necessarily mean not communicating or understanding each other less. Rather, it is more a process of sharing in contrast to the "shutting out" aspect of spoken language. In silence we attend to more things. In silence we see the past, present and future.

In speech we fix things in time which is usually the immediate present. Speech is a futile act of "momentary immortality." A cry of, "I exist." Silence is a consciousness of our relation to both time and timelessness. It is the infinite and the speck of dust at the same time. Silence is many dimensional, multi-sensual. Speech, in its categorical, ordering fashion, can only convey some of the experiences of the five senses. Silence is the total experience of the five senses and more. It also includes so-called "extra-sensory perception," which we in our futility, also try to describe with words.

Words by necessity quantify concepts that in life cannot be measured or compared. How can one gauge "less versus more freedom?" "Beautiful, more beautiful, most beautiful?"

VII.

Speaking is a form of experience. But it need not replace silence. Words are necessary but not to give a sense of order. Silence is not the absence of words. It is not a void that is to be filled. For even the word silence is wrong. Poets listen to the sounds of silence. Words are to enhance experiences, not to limit them. That means less syntax and semantics, and more of the so-called "vegetable salad" of schizophrenic speech. We shall understand one another by expanding on each other's experiences—not by reducing our experiences to the same common elements in standardized words.

There is more than one way to say "hello," more than one way to say, "I love you," and no ways to say freedom. The moment we reduce a multi-dimensional, multi-sensual experience to one spoken word, we destroy the infinite richness surrounding us. We castrate the imagination of man and impose a totalitarian order. We have imprisoned the world with words. In the process we have also become prisoners of our own words.

October 25, 1986, Marburg

NO LONGER FREE: MADNESS IN MODERN TIMES

IV

Mickey Mouse

MAIN STREET
FANTASYLAND
ADVENTURELAND
FRONTIERLAND

There's no doubt that fate can save you from your illness better than I can. But if I can manage to convert your hysterical pains to a common misery, you too can convince yourself that you have benefited.
Sigmund Freud

I.

We have witnessed the standardization of even madness in the 20th century. That which by definition should fall outside the domain of structured society is now so much with us that the so-called "mad" are expected to meticulously follow all bureaucratic procedures and niceties in order to get appointments and meet the fees of professional healers. Madness is a part of today's totalitarian evolving state. The official healers, psychiatrists and psychologists, licensed to practice by the state, determine that which is to be called madness. The mad are losing the freedom of their madness.

II.

The ultimate in madness is a unique vision of reality, of the order of things. A radically different way of looking at the relations between things. The ultimate point in its freedom however is its individuality. Although, as Shakespeare said, there may be a method to madness, that method changes from one particular individual to another. Even anarchists rally around a mutually accepted black flag, have goals, restrictions and symbols which they hold in common. There is a code, a standard for an anarchist to uphold, otherwise (s)he shall be excluded. It is only the mad who are unburdened of a communal straightjacket.

All follow their own tune, a tune that one may change whenever one wishes and still pursue a particular path of madness. The practice of psychiatry has taken this, the most ultimate of freedoms, away. Madness has been declared to be an illness just like appendicitis, measles or cancer. This is the modern view in place of the Middle Age's belief in lunacy. Then, the individual was believed to be affected by forces over which even the most supreme force in society—God—had lost his influence. Thus, implicitly madness was considered to be a force equal to the highest in our spiritual realm. After the Enlightenment, the Industrial Revolution and positivism, madness fell under the same category as the common cold—an illness to be cured by one of thousands of practitioners. The more modern view is that the whole staff of the psychiatric hospital, from the doctor to the nurse, the social worker and down to the attendant is a member of the therapeutic team that can deal with mental illness. A far cry from the mightiness of lunacy in the European Middle Ages that required not only the highest authority of the church, but also its most devout and honoured members in inquisitions. Not being able to overcome lunacy was tantamount to the weakness of god. The furthest the supreme authority in the Middle Ages could go was to ask the mad either to repent or to at least admit that they had been under the influence of the fallen angel Lucifer. In the 18th and 19th centuries the mad were kept in asylums. Our modern order no longer fears the mad. They are merely marginalized as undesirable.

III.

Madness has been reduced to the common cold so that it no longer poses a threat to the establishment. The state has become more totalitarian contiguously with madness having lost its individuality and imagination. The more it has come under the domain of the state, the more it has lost its freedom. The state has castrated madness by calling it an illness. It has standardized madness by defining it, by categorizing it.

The official definers of madness, the American Psychiatric Association (APA), whose views effect most countries, rules over the Kingdom of Madness. In a sense, they have followed the dictum that a good general is one who gives orders that he knows will be obeyed. Thus, the American Psychiatric Association has kept ahead of all potential sources of opposition. The professional mental health community for example, no longer considers women to be intellectually inferior as they did in the early twentieth century. Had they done so, they would have lost all political control, which is the ultimate source of their power rather than science or knowledge. They changed, of course, because of the Suffragette movement and the women's right to vote. The mental health community has been adept at assimilating all potential forces of opposition before they have become threatening to the establishment's definition of sanity, the establishment's right to define sanity itself.

In the same vein, it was decided by the APA in the 70's that homosexuality was no longer to be considered a mental illness. A certain type of behaviour and personality that for years had been in abnormal psychology textbooks and in the education programs for psychiatrists went from being abnormal to normal overnight. Why? There had been no "scientific" argument for this change. Of course, there had also been no scientific argument when homosexuality was first classed as a mental disease/behavioural disorder. What had forced the decision was the development and the growing political power of the gay liberation movement. In all those cases where the opposition has had potential political strength, the establishment has changed its sanity criteria.

Such flexibility has given it even greater political power. Thus, not only do they continue their unchallenged position to judge on madness, but at the same time, with each act of assimilation, as in the case of women and homosexuals, they increase the number of their adherents and supporters while further legitimizing the establishment's right to rule on madness.

IV.

Of all the oppressed, we are least concerned with the mad. Vietnam in the 1960's, Suffragette movement of the 1930's, Blacks in the U.S. and South Africa, gay liberation, anti-nuclear movement, animal rights, etc. have had worldwide enthusiastic backing. All the above have been popular with intellectuals. Yet, for the most suppressed there has been no action. Why?

Simply because we are all prejudiced against the mad. They make us uneasy. We also do not even know what the unifying call of protest should be. "U.S. out of Vietnam," "No to apartheid" were slogans in keeping with the context. What does one demand for the so called mad?

One would think that the most basic appeal would be to remove those restraints that make the "mad" the most oppressed. That is, they should be able to enjoy their civil rights. As the matter stands, it's not even the judicial system but the psychiatrist, his oppressor, who decides on the enjoyment or the curtailment of such rights. For the patient's so-called benefit. The psychiatrist has the power to restrain the so-called patient's freedom of speech, freedom of travel and freedom of organization. Those in a mental hospital often cannot make a phone call without the express permission of the psychiatrist. In the overcrowded mental hospitals, many do not even get to see the psychiatrist except when he makes his express rounds, as if inspecting a multitude of tomato plants. Some are confined to their wards for years, many do not even see sunlight. Whether they are able to write or receive letters, who can visit them, how frequently and when, is determined by the psychiatrist. Such decisions are usually made on a mass basis as the hospitals are understaffed. Never mind knowing his case on an individual basis, (the basis and justification of psychiatry and its model of treatment), the psychiatrist may not even be aware of the number of patients that (s)he is responsible for.

No one takes action for freedom and civil rights on behalf of the mad in mental hospitals. Yet, of all the oppressed, they are the only ones who cannot, are not allowed to, do not have the freedom to appeal their case. At most, their complaint will be judged by yet another psychiatrist. They can't hold press conferences, demonstrations, they can't even vote or make use of their own private property as they please.

Although we can discuss for hours a book by Nietzsche, a painting by Van Gogh, or the fine points of epileptic seizures in Dostoyevsky, we are all very uneasy should we be with a mad person for any period of time. Even a moment together. We are afraid of the unexpected that might happen. The mad are expected to do unexpected things. We do not know how to deal with the unexpected. We like to predict and control things in our professional, social and sexual relationships. (What we really can't control are our dreams which we either forget or repress.) It is not that there will be physical harm done to us when we are with the mad, or with any person in a state of madness. (Statistics show that the mad are less prone to violence than "ordinary" individuals in society.) Rather, we fear the unexpected. He may tear his clothes off, start singing a childish song, begin to speak in parables, just sit there and say nothing, show brotherly affection, make sexual advances. He may do any or none of these. But we, who are on our guard, all fear him. His unstructured, free, indeterminate behaviour for us is a situation that we do not know how to deal with. Our need to control, of course, is a sign of totalitarianism in each and every one of us. Completely free, unstructured situations bother us. Just like silence. Silence disturbs us. Being with the mad is the same. There are no previously agreed upon rules. Only that which can be spontaneous.

V.

Psychiatry is perhaps the only scientific profession in modern times that can stand on its own without its success or efficiency being measured by any criteria. If a surgeon consistently fails in his operations and kills his patients, he will obviously lose his job. A bus driver who is not able to drive a bus properly, a soldier who can't shoot, a politician who can't win elections, an academician with no accepted publications, a cook whose food is not edible, a prostitute who is frigid are all failures. Yet in psychiatry there is no research proving that therapy is effective (as versus no therapy) or that one method of therapy is more effective than another. Although psychiatrists and psychologists have tried for years to undertake research to prove the viability of psychiatry, to prove that those who go to a psychiatrist have a greater chance of getting "well" than those who don't, they have not succeeded. In short, in terms of its stated goals, psychiatry doesn't work.

As a profession and professionals, however, they hold a prestigious place in society. In many countries they are one of the highest paid professions. They command the utmost respect from almost everybody. People feel uneasy and anxious before them. Former U.S. President Nixon, when he was running for election, wanted to make sure that during his campaign there would be no psychiatrists who would be in a position to meet him. Those who don't fear to wage war and bomb other people, fear psychiatrists. Whenever I used to tell someone that I was a psychologist, one of the first reactions would be, "Oh, I have to watch out what I say to you." The psychiatrist is the policeman par excellence in today's totalitarian society. There is no right of appeal against his opinion claiming that one does not fit the norms of society, that one is mad. He can only be questioned by yet another psychiatrist. His power is not limited to the authority vested on him by the establishment. We as individuals also reaffirm his power. No matter how free we say we are, no matter how much we say we can do anything we want, we still fear to go beyond the norms, fear to be told with one look and word of the psychiatrist, that we are not normal.

We are afraid to be free. We want to stay within the establishment-dictated, mutually accepted bounds of behaviour and attitude. We dare not take that step to ultimate independence, to listen to the tune of our own drummer. When we do, we are usually called mad. We don't want to be called mad. We don't have the strength to face the consequences of being called mad and treated as mad. Therefore, we castrate what we mean by madness and reduce it to petty acts, while at the same time exaggerating the meaning of our attempts at unorthodox behaviour. For example, a father stays at home from work one day for the only reason that the weather is beautiful and he wants to go out and fly a kite. "I wonder if they'll call me mad," he thinks. Or afterwards, when he's relating the incident. "I did such a crazy thing..." We have reduced madness to simple acts so that we can safely be mad, have our cake and eat it too. "We stayed up all night and listened to the night, wasn't that absolutely mad?" "My husband turned on all the lights, opened all the windows and made love to me on the rug in our living room. How mad we must have been. Imagine me giving way to such craziness." "You are crazy," she muttered as he rolled on top of her while the other overnight guests were soundly asleep in the same room. Because we dare not be mad and yet still yearn for freedom, we have reduced madness to mean those very simple acts of behaviour which do injustice to the infinite expressions of madness.

VI.

The role of the psychiatrist is oppressive. His duty is to help people conform to the norms and standards set by the ruling elite. Whether he is successful in his work with the individual is of no great importance for society. If he is "successful," the "patient" returns to society as a docile, co-operative citizen. If the psychiatrist is unsuccessful, the "patient" is ostracized, either locked up and put away in a hospital or drugged up and banished to the streets. Either way, the patient will not be a danger in terms of going against society, showing his individual non-standard behaviour before others.

The role of the psychiatrist is oppressive because his primary interest is not in the health or so-called sanity of the individual. His main obligation is to uphold the accepted standards of behaviour established by the ruling elite, class, party or culture. In upholding such standards, the psychiatrist reinforces those very institutions that limit man's growth and freedom. A very clear-cut illustration is the role of the military psychiatrist. When a soldier too frightened to fight and kill others is brought to him, the obligation of the psychiatrist is to send him back to battle as soon as possible. From the psychiatrist's point of view and from the point of view of the forces he represents, what is normal is for the soldier to carry out his function as a killer. What is abnormal is for him to be frightened, not to want to fight, not to want to kill. The duty of the psychiatrist is to make him, as soon as possible, a killer again. It is never the duty of the psychiatrist, it has never been the duty of the psychiatrist to question the sanity of their "leaders" who have made the decision for war, the decision that others should be killed, the decision that may perhaps lead to the end of the species homo sapiens and many other species along with us.

There is a field of psychology, military psychology, whose main task is to look for those psychological principles and methods that will enable armies and soldiers to be more efficient instruments of killing. Along with other scientists, they hold their annual scientific meetings, share the same prestige, receive more money for research and are usually better paid than their colleagues. There is no field of peace psychology.

VII.

The trend in modern times has been for madness to become increasingly rationalized. Here we must differentiate between collective and individual madness. Collective madness is that order and system of values which is espoused by the state and its institutions. Those individuals who do not hear their own tune, who fear to follow their drummer, give in to identifying with the follies of the state. A good citizen is one who is part of the collective madness. Collective madness is destructive. The globalization and standardization of the economy along with its dressing and eating habits, sexual norms, entertainment and arts is increasingly leading to one big collective unit that dominates life in all its aspects. Erich Fromm called this the making of a mega-machine and saw in it a new and much more enhancing type of fascism.

In this new evolving order, individual madness is constrained not so much by law, the police and the judges but rather by ourselves. We have feelings of fear and guilt acting as a brake with respect to our potential actions as individuals. We are also attracted by the collective frenzy of the crowd. For both, stopping at red lights or lynching an enemy of the people are acts of compliance and a mutually shared frenzy.

The whole world system is built on mad assumptions rationalized by laws, consumer patterns, economical theories, religion and other similar constructs.

Consider the classic story of the Welsh coalminer's son.

"Mother, I am cold. Can't you light the stove?"

"We have no coal."

"Why?"

"Because we have no money."

"Why?"

"Because your father has lost his job."

"Why?"

"Because there is too much coal."

Such madness is the order of things under capitalism. In most cases the madness is accepted a priori.

One important characteristic of collective madness, and what can keep it going for centuries, is that it cannot be changed collectively. That is, collective action against collective madness leads only to further collective madness.

A most prime and recent example is the Soviet Revolution. In the name of making a revolution on behalf of the poor, nearly 20 million peasants were, in official revolutionary terminology, liquidated. In the name of freeing the mind and intellect from the shackles of capitalism, thousands of intellectuals were liquidated. It is madness that in the name of freedom there is no right of speech, travel and assembly. There is also no right to life. The state kills.

The French Revolution is another example of a collective madness replaced by yet another form of collective madness. The state replaced the church. Totalitarian state education replaced totalitarian religious education. A new class came to power. Only to repeat the same collective madness all over again. The new power structure called for new enemies.

Just as there were those who were a threat to religion, now there were those considered a threat to the state. The structure, by definition, necessitates an enemy. It cannot but have enemies. In circumstances where they cannot survive because of brutal physical and psychological suppression, then enemies must be found, created, provoked, or even imagined. More examples of collective madness: In the 1950's in the U.S., at the height of the McCarthy era, children looked for communists under their beds before going to sleep. Now, we are all looking for terrorists, rarely bothering to look at our mad, self-destructive global state of affairs.

Intellectuals like to point to the Third Reich and National Socialism in Germany as an aberration in human society. It is agreed by many that this is indeed a case of collective madness. For it was not just a matter of a gang of thugs or one mad man ruling a country, but rather the people (workers, intellectuals, women, the young, the elderly) sharing a common frenzy. How can we be so foolish to think that this is a phenomenon particular to only one people at one place and time in history? Yet we are. For we fail to recognize the collective madness in our very own beliefs, behaviour and history.

Horkheimer, Adorno and their friends escaped from fascism in Germany to the U.S. There, they carried out a study on anti-semitism. They found that it was much higher in the U.S. after Hitler than it had been in Germany before Hitler came to power. Throughout history there are many examples of people criticizing totalitarian orders in other societies, yet supporting racist, chauvinistic, totalitarian systems of their own. What is of less dramatic interest is the collective madness that we uphold in our daily lives. We spend millions on manufacturing and buying faster and faster cars and at the same time keep on controlling and decreasing the speed limits. With utmost politeness we offer poison to each other in the form of cigarettes and the state gets a commission from each sale. In Turkey, the Air Force gets a percentage from each killing cigarette sale so that they can buy even more killer planes and killer bombs.

Although there is plenty of space to live in the world, we have come so close together as to require traffic lights to order us to know when to walk and stop. In many modern cities people are known to have killed for a parking spot.

We accept this collective madness to such a degree that our understanding is a criterion for intelligence. Thus, in the most widely used intelligence test in the world, the following is asked, "Why does land in the city cost more than land in the country?" The rationalization of this mad collective order is taken as a sign of intelligence.

Madness has become incorporated in intelligence tests, in economical theories, in international law and in everyday behaviour. While the psychiatrist helps us restrict, restrain our individual madness, he also guides us toward adjusting to and sharing the totalitarian collective madness. His job is to make us conform to society. Society has no time to think. It is always on the move. When some individuals who cannot stand the pace or the strain drop out, when those individuals who are the idolized pace-setters die, other immediately take their place. Not moving at the pace of society, not adapting to its current and ever changing standards is for the psychiatrist and for us a sign of psychological problems. The person going to the psychiatrist in this sense is like a race car being serviced at the pit before it gets back on the track. The race is not questioned. It is those who question the race that are questioned by the psychiatrist.

VIII.

It is collective madness at its height that is most against individual madness. The first people to be systematically killed under German totalitarianism were the so-called mad, the mentally ill, the insane. They were also the only segment of society who did not join the collective madness. Many others who were originally anti-fascist eventually changed sides. The mad did not because it was psychologically impossible. Individual madness is individually specific.

The only way to oppose the totalitarianism of collective madness is through the individual. The richness of the homo sapiens is in the heterogeneity of its members — the individual has infinite combinations of creativity and looking at the universe. This heterogeneity is a safeguard for the survival of our species. The species, any species, can basically survive for eons in spite of drastic environmental changes because of the variety within the species. Those members who adjust to or fit the drastic changes in the environment continue to survive and through them the species. Variety is needed for survival.

Biologically however, we are becoming more and more standardized. Through controlling the environment and also standardizing it (same temperature at home, in the car, and at the work place through air conditioning and heating machines, same types of food and habits of eating, sleeping, same types of medicine—especially penicillin) we are biologically becoming more and more uniform and as a result, a weaker species. However, we still have a chance for biological survival because we can control and change our environment. (The danger here of course is that we may, in our efforts to control, ultimately destroy the ecological system and thereby the possibility for any kind of life.)

Another threat to the survival of the homo sapiens (and the planet) is the psychological standardization of man. Politics, economics, education, entertainment are now all dominated from a few centers all controlled by the same powers. Local cultures, hitherto unaffected, have now become targets of the new totalitarianism. It was once enough to be a loyal consumer of products. Beyond that one could do whatever one liked. Now, that space is also falling under the domain of the forces from the center. One's sexual behaviour, relation to time and work, attitudes with respect to the planets, cars, birds, paradigms of thinking, are all to be in accordance with set standards.

Thus, the variety in human behaviour with respect to all its aspects ranging from type of sexual activity to paradigms of thinking is becoming one-fold. People are to be judged against a world consumer's standard totalitarian criterion of normalcy.

Our psychological differentiation is important for our survival on two grounds. First, as a guarantee against totalitarianism. The more the society allows for individual madness, the less there will be who will participate in collective madness. Second, as a guarantee to see us through the unexpectedness of the coming centuries. With the explosion of knowledge and our increasing flirtation with infinity and the unknowns of the universe, we need to protect as much individual variation as possible. Robots and the most sophisticated computers may fail utterly in reacting to previously unknown phenomena. Individual madness, the chance for the individual to reach his utmost potential of expression, increases the ingenuity and the creativity of the species to react to, and build on different situations.

IX.

The standardization of man, madness, and freedom in the twentieth century has removed any sense of intensity in life itself. Nothing is intensely felt. There is no time for depth. All experiences must be fleeting. Experiences are like chattel—to be bought or gotten ridden of, to be experienced at will. We choose experience as if buying something from a department store. It is rumored that Dostoyevsky suffered from intense guilt feelings because of a sexual act he's said to have had with a female child. He was tormented throughout his life. A hundred years later, travel agencies book sex tours for Germans, Japanese and Americans so that they can be flown into Manila or Bangkok and have as much sex with as many child prostitutes as they wish for the duration of their journey. In a week they are comfortably back at their jobs and secure in their environments. Consumed experience extinguishes the spirit.

It is becoming more and more possible for us to experience almost anything in specially constructed environments, as in the case of sex tourism. Thus, with the right contacts, one could also partake in a witchcraft ceremony including actual sacrifice, participate in an expedition to the North Pole, live like a feudal lord in a British manor and on and on. All this, while continuing to work as a priest, mailman or psychologist. There is no risk, no sense of being in a situation where the end is not certain. You are usually even guaranteed to have a good time, to enjoy it, to have a thrill.

The totalitarianism of controlled experience is accompanied by poverty of imagination. Even at "good" Western restaurants, the menu and the waiter are similar to the warder and regulations in a prison. "You can have two vegetables with this meal," "No salad comes with that order." In eating out one has the "freedom to choose" from an increasingly restricted multiple choice list. Eating, an important source of pleasure for man, is a controlled experience. So is sex. Rather than the infinity of experience, we are face to face with assortments of sex paraphernalia, sex-machines (vibrators) various fixed patterns that standardize and limit our sense of pleasure. Eating, sex, madness have all been broken down into categories. The total experience is no longer. Rather, one chooses a set pattern of experience from a limited multiple choice set.

X.

The anti-hero of civilization will be the mad person. In spite of the permeation of standardization and totalitarianism, those who can still be mad are indeed very strong and unique individuals. One should not use the word "mad" lightly, for there are very few who can be accorded that privilege. It is a privilege accompanied by great suffering. It is a suffering that is rarely alleviated. The path of the mad is so lonely that although he may have empathy with the world and the cosmos, he is also beyond praise and punishment.

The mad are alone against the totalitarian state which is built upon the totalitarianism in each and every one of us. They are also under the potential threat of the complete standardization of madness through "breakthroughs" in bio-chemical technology and perhaps genetical engineering. If we cannot protect ourselves, let us at least, in the name of the human spirit, allow the mad to be free in their madness.

October 31, 1986, Marburg

HERE WE EAT, THERE WE SLEEP

V

Doan's Playhouse, 1991

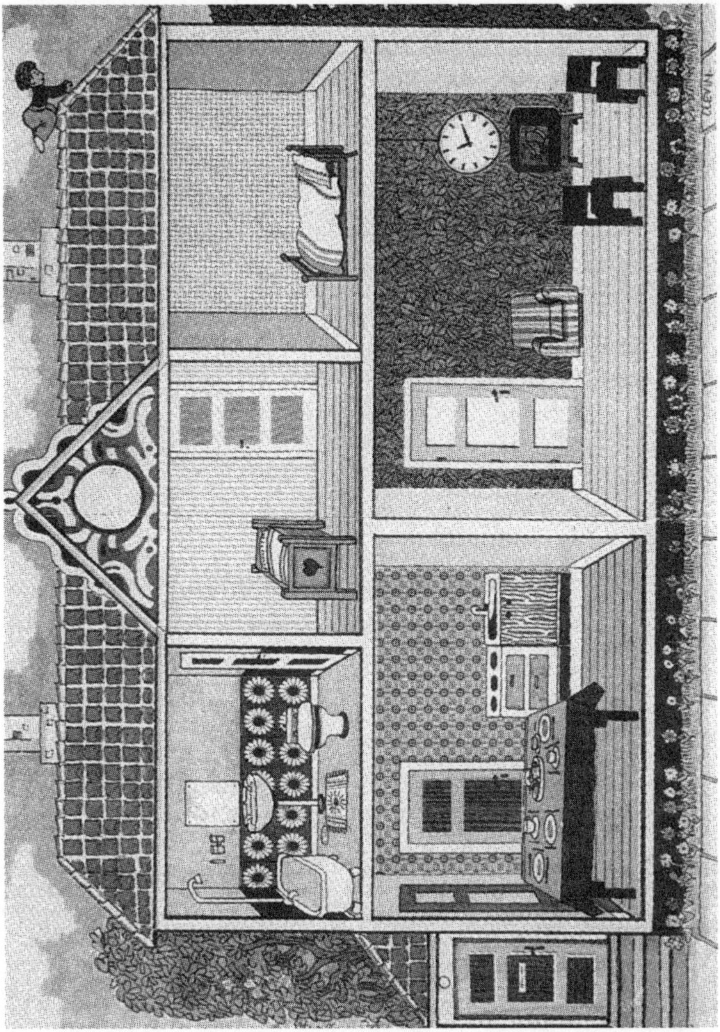

Countess: But why drink so much?
Antonio: That's what separates us from animals Madame; to drink when we are not thirsty and to make love when we want.
Beaumarchais

I.

The classic house/apartment of our time is divided into various quarters. Each area is based on a certain function of the body. Thus, there is a sitting (living) room for sitting, dining room for eating, bedroom for sleeping, bathroom for washing and defecating, kitchen for cooking.

The reaction of recent architecture has been to at least open the walls, tear them down so that there will be as much human contact as possible between spaces. But the use of space is still totalitarian. What should be done where, and even how it should be done is ordered. In corresponding to the various functions of the body, the contemporary living space divides and rules, whereas the human is a whole and multifunctional organism.

II.

The specialized space-efficient apartment is a totalitarian arrangement. It results in millions living exactly the same way with the same motions, subject to the same identical environments. It leads to the breaking up of any sense of community under the same roof, since it is the specialized arrangement of space that dictates what should be done and where.

It hinders any act of creativity to rearrange the use of space. It sets a false example of reality by creating a sense of order in the environment where everything has its proper place. In summary, the apartment is to us what the barrack is to the soldier. The barracks, as an extension of the uniform, instill a sense of unquestioned discipline. The same is now true for our living space. We, in our century, have become civilian soldiers living in apartment barracks.

The space-efficient apartments of recent origin, reflects the utmost in the totalitarianism of living space. When looked in from the outside, one often sees that all TV sets are in the same place in one apartment building after another. The couch where one sits to watch television is also in the same place. We eat, defecate and have sex exactly in the same surroundings. It is very simple for a complete stranger to walk into a flat and find everything as if he had been living there for years. The living spaces of today no longer reflect the individual nor the cultural differences of their occupants. The same building could be anywhere in the world. Such totalitarian living space forces all creativity in the human, in terms of ordering his environment, to be nullified, desensitized.

III.

The totalitarian home of our times, in addition to functionally ordering space, also lacks the freest space of all. Almost all homes have had their secret place in the form of an attic and sometimes the cellar. For many still, the attic has many rich, wild, nostalgic, secret colourful associations. Not only was it a place for perfect disorder, but it also signified historical continuity from one generation to another. There were many things from those who once lived, many newspapers, letters, photographs, all a testimony to things as they were. Attics could very quickly bring history to life, to the present. A major threat to the totalitarian state which aims to form people to always fit the needs of the immediate present is a sense of history. The destruction of the attic is the eradication of history in the home. Grandmother's sole teddy in the bedroom or a photograph album are now mere anachronisms.

IV.

A specialized division of function in a house keeps a family or the people living there apart. Multi-function use of the same space keeps the family together. In traditional Swedish kitchens where all ate together, there is a wooden bench for the father to light his pipe, then to doze off a bit while the mother and the children are doing the dishes. The point is not the sex of the person who naps but rather the fact that people stick together. In our modern efficient kitchen there is no room for such a bench. Eliminated, not just because our century does not condone the man sleeping while the woman is doing the dishes, but because the space is oriented to mechanical efficiency rather than human activity.

Speed, function and efficiency have become so important in the home that human engineers carry out time and motion studies in designing efficient living space just as if they were designing submarines or airplane cockpits. If they can afford it, there are even separate bathrooms for the modern husband and wife. Not having such dual facilities is often a source of argument between many couples. Why? Because they hinder each other's speed and efficiency both in the functional process of things related to the bathrooms and with respect to their concept of "lifestyle." (There was once a time when the wooden tub would be before all to see, and the family would scrub each other down, often with laughter, joy and tender love and care.)

Space also orders our sense of privacy. It is considered wrong, for instance, that children be in the same space in which the parents sleep and love. Rather, the family fears even discussing such matters. We sleep behind closed and sometimes even locked doors. A closed door policy also opens the door for the state to step into our private lives. It becomes the duty of the central unit of power –the government– to teach its young the ways of sex—a utilitarian mechanistic undertaking with the aim of reducing population growth, preventing unwanted pregnancies and securing hygienic sex—all of which have nothing to do with love.

V.

Not only do the rooms define what we should do in them, but they also effect both our mental state and the manner of relationships that we have with others. Should you be sitting in the study in the middle of the day, it would be considered that you are thinking/contemplating. The same behaviour in the bedroom would be considered resting or just being plain lazy. There are feelings and types of conditioning associated with each room. Such conditions prevent one from thinking at length about any specific subject or having deeper relations with anyone else. The various functional rooms keep all thoughts, conversations, feelings and relationships as near to the function as possible. Going from room to room changes our mental set. It is like going from one country, one culture to another. In each room we have a different function. Accordingly, we are divided and ruled by the totalitarian structure of the living space. In contrast, being in undefined space is accompanied by heightened concentration, relaxation and peace. It results in introspection, allows for creativity and ingenuity. One learns to make various uses for the same space, instead of the functional spaces commanding a person what to do.

The ordering of living space gives order to our emotions. When on a visit to another house, if you are received in the bedroom your feelings will be different than if you are received in the living room, which will still be different than being received in the kitchen. Accordingly, the topic of conversation, the limits of intimacy, will be determined more by the space than by ourselves. The same applies to the dining room. Certain conversations considered improper for the dining room are perfectly entertaining in the living room. Bedrooms are only for sleeping and each to his own bed! Those who a few minutes ago were very close and intimate in the dining room or the living room, sitting close, touching each other in the act of conversation must now be separated by walls. Though people perfectly strange to each other can dance intimately at discos and ballrooms, they cannot be so intimate or even close in the quarters of their own homes, lest it be "misunderstood."

VI.

With respect to most of our behaviour we seem to be on a path leading to the extinction of our species. The standard apartment unit of our century is an example. A bird's nest, which is the result of instinctive behaviour, shows more variation and use of natural surroundings than the block apartments we are building throughout the world today.

Today's standard living units induce in us fixed action patterns accompanied by uniform mental sets. An environment that does not show change and variety dulls not only the individual but also negatively affects the development of our species. The totalitarianism in our living space is not only a sign of our enslavement to fixed standards, it may also be a threat to the existence of our species.

Over 2000 years have passed since the last Greek symposium. Eating, drinking, listening to music, dancing and lying on couches and discussing philosophy in the free reign of spontaneity. All in the same space!

November 6, 1986, Marburg

HEROES ARE TOTALITARIAN

VI

The shame of the Corsican creature, James Ensor, 1891

What's a throne? A piece of shiny wood covered with cloth.
I am the state. Here, I am the sole representative of the people.
Even if I had made a mistake, you should not have criticized me before them.
People wash their dirty laundry at home.
France needs me more than I need France.
Napoleon Bonaparte

I.

Our history has been an attempt to avoid freedom. On the whole we have been trying to adjust rather than resist or create. Those few who do, and even sacrifice their lives, become lies and legends about what we are not. Heroes, as the embodiment of such lies, are evidence of our wish for enslavement. Not daring to live in freedom, we delegate it to heroes whom we worship. Heroes are characteristic of the totalitarianism in us. They are also an absolute must for totalitarian regimes.

II.

All societies, groups, religions, movements have had their heroes. The hero of the Soviet Revolution, Lenin, is embalmed and lying in Red Square. There are rumours that the embalmed body may not even be that of Lenin. The 20th century did not know the secret of embalming as the ancient Egyptians did. Why should a socialist state believing in the forces of history and the power of the masses insist on keeping a hero "alive"? The capitalist states also have their heroes, but in their case they usually keep on changing them like consumer items in order to be able to enforce their own type of oppression. They discover heroes, they manufacture heroes, and overnight, they kill their heroes through the very efficient and controlled use of the mass media.

Religions too have their heroes. Believers swear in the name of their heroes, die in their name, bless their children in their name. If democracy, if all the isms, if religion are based on principles and ideas, and if in over forty centuries plus of civilization, society is more educated as we claim, then why do we still have one dimensional heroes so much removed from life? Both because of our own totalitarian tendency and because of the need for the establishment to exploit this tendency. Legendary figures in folk tales, in contrast to the heroes of the establishment, are always in everyday surroundings confronted with everyday affairs. Many are portrayed with their so called weaknesses. That we use such a word as "weakness" is sign enough that our generally accepted image of the hero is totalitarian. Otherwise, why use the word "weakness" to describe what is a common, normal characteristic in all of us?

The ancient Greeks were a freer society with their mythological Gods who had human "weaknesses." The almighty Zeus was a henpecked husband. Since then, heroes have come a long way, more and more managed by the forces that rule us.

III.

The "human" in the hero is of no use to the totalitarian order. We too, hold no special esteem for the "human." We do for the hero. The hero is not human. Except for his heroic deed and all else seen in its halo, the less known about him the better. The totalitarian order retires from the public eye its "one act" heroes before they can show their human face and become embarrassing. For the hero, to be kept alive, must live only in people's imagination. Thus, for instance, heroes are always imagined to be bigger than they really are. One of our most common reactions upon encountering a hero is to exclaim our surprise at not having found him as big as we had imagined him to be.

Use of technology has facilitated the establishment's manipulation of the hero. The image of today's hero is controlled especially via television and photographs. Months can pass (and, maybe in the future years) before anyone from the public can actually see the hero in person or talk with someone who has. The everyday life of the hero not related to his heroism is censored. We usually know absolutely nothing about such things as the hero's snoring, disagreements with his mother, his jokes, bad breath, blushing or how (s)he wakes up in the morning. Such details would be the beginning of the humanization and therefore the death of the hero. The word scandal, as applied to the hero, usually means that he has been "caught" by us in the act of being human. That we drink, gamble, commit adultery, laugh, lie, cry, and blush –which we do not allow our hero– is further evidence of seeing the normal in us as a weakness. We show a duplicity not only in creating the hero and isolating him but worse yet, battering him on his downfall for showing human "weaknesses." The more we think we are "just human," the stronger is need for making him even mightier.

Heroes are used to disguise that which is natural. The ambivalent nature of society and man is not reflected upon our one dimensional heroes. In contrast to the hero, we can do contradictory things. The hero must be consistent.

A traitor to one country is a hero to another. This was

held especially in the Soviet Union and the United States. But a person who criticizes the lack of freedom in both societies (as in the case of Svetlana, Stalin's daughter who first defected to the U.S. then back to the Soviet Union and then to England) cannot be a hero to any society. For all societies have false heroes. Heroes are as clearly defined and as standardized as a McDonald's hamburger. The hero in all his details must meet with all the prejudices and value judgments of society. Thus, with the greatest Christian hero, Jesus. In his portrayals, his skin and eye colour change as a function of where his image is exhibited. Thus, in Scandinavia Jesus is a blue-eyed blond Saxon. In the Mediterranean he is a dark skinned Semite. How many Christians have the image of a circumcised Jesus? All the attributes of a hero must meet the ideals, values, doctrines of the establishment of the ruling class(es). There must be nothing ambivalent or ambiguous about him. All images of those who are presented to us as heroes are totalitarian.

Until we accept ourselves as we are, we shall continue to create heroes, supermen and gods to imprison us. A hero has no place in free society.

A free person has no heroes.

IV.

Without heroes we are individuals. With heroes we are a group. Individuals have consciences and principles. Groups adjust and have laws. Individually we live, collectively we survive. A cat sheds its fur in the summer and grows a thick coat in the winter in the process of adjusting to the environment so that it can continue to survive. With "the passing of seasons" we too survive by changing heroes and ideologies. How and how much we change is a function of our obeying and adjusting as a crowd. Resisting on the basis of principles is not important for the continuation of our species. We survive by adjusting collectively. We "live" by asserting individually. Not believing in ourselves, not having the strength to assert our individuality, we go along with the group.

The psychologist Asch showed that a string shorter than others was always referred to as being longer by the experimental subject, just because all others before him (as part of the experimental design) had pointed out the shorter string as being longer. After the experiment all admitted that in spite of knowing the string was shorter they had gone along with the group decision.

Whether a state exerts brutal physical force or makes use of psychological manipulation is particular to the type of totalitarianism. What is of primary importance is that we obey. With heroes, not only do we obey but we also follow unquestioningly. Yet we do not obey like circus animals. We rationalize so as not to see our contradictions. A military dictator coming on the wake of a destabilized democracy is often cheered by the same people who only weeks before belonged to and voted for the now discredited political parties. We fear, obey and survive.

Adorno, Arendt, Horkheimer, and the Frankfurt School were completely off the mark when they tried to find in people either a democratic or an authoritarian personality. Their undertaking reflected the sides of World War II. The fascists were said to have authoritarian personalities. Those who opposed them were democratic. Simple as that. Later research in North America showed that the Americans, whom they had thought to be democratic, were more antisemitic even after the war than the Germans had been before the war. That which is bad is more a function of who the enemy is, than a matter of the enemy's characteristics or personality.

Bronfenbrenner showed for instance that the Americans and the Russians have a mirror image of each other. They think of each other in the same terms—bad. Dostoyevski showed us that we are both good and bad. One step further would be to say we are what we are. Heroes are not what we are.

V.

Heroes are so totalitarian that once created they can become problematic, even after their death. A totalitarian society creates and recognizes its hero within the context of a specific period. Changes in leadership inevitably lead to renunciation of some past heroes. A typical example is the Soviet Union where the burial wall around the Kremlin was at one time the scene of a game of "musical graves." In accordance with changes in the power structure, the hero's grave was either removed or brought back.

That we delegate deeds to the hero and in turn take a spectator's seat is clearly evident when they are demoted or dead. We adjust just as much to the exploits of the hero as we do to his downfall. We support the hero when he is strong, disown him when he is weak. Neither his rise nor fall has anything to do with what the hero does, but rather with what we make of him.

A hero revered by millions, can be disowned by the same millions overnight. We have seen many examples of this in history. The most prominent example from our century is perhaps the People's Republic of China and Chairman Mao. Almost overnight (though after his death) the type of socialism he stood for was condemned by the new regime with the apparent full backing of the most populous nation-state in the world—over one billion people. We saw a radical change in the leadership and the politics of China. The same billion who had once fanatically waved and religiously quoted from Mao's Red Book of Quotations began to cheer a leader with almost the opposite stand saying, "It doesn't matter that a cat is white or black, as long as it catches the mouse."

Heroes are often used to convey messages to the people on the assumption that what is associated with the hero can only be good. Thus matters ranging from raising internal loans to going to war often use the same image of the great hero in their appeal to the people. The absolute farce in manipulating heroes occurs when rulers bring in the images of their respective national heroes in order to attempt and justify new political relationships. I have seen comparisons of the same nation-state hero Ataturk with George Washington, Lenin and Hitler. In each case similarities between his and the other great leader's image were discussed by academicians and statesmen alike. We are both the creators and the audience in this ridiculous farce.

No matter what their "cry," heroes inevitably and inadvertently serve the forces of totalitarianism. A hero who rises against the forces of oppression is, in his entity as a hero, also a force of oppression. An example of such a hero is Spartacus. Through his execution the ruling powers are able to put an end to the forces of rebellion. Heroes like Spartacus, heroes like Che fulfill the needs of the establishment. They provoke. As they are colourful figures, men with uncompromising resolution, they are attractive to the oppressed. Some of the oppressed (at the beckoning of the hero) go with the hero. In the end, they are all cut down. The opposition is pacified and, what's worse, the people's will is broken.

VI.

A hero, in all languages, cultures and religions has positive connotations. It is a good thing to be. Children between the ages of eight and twelve like stories about heroes. Whether the hero is a cowboy, a football player, soldier, gangster or a ballet dancer is not important. Children admire, daydream, and also "nightdream" of becoming heroes.

Both the forces of the establishment and the various forces of opposition encourage, feed and exploit this characteristic in children. They employ their writers to write hero stories. Communists write stories about brave children fighting the enemies of the people, capitalists have their "rags to riches" heroes, Jesuits tell tales about the lives of the saints, nation-states worship their liberators.

Public relations agents representing sports figures, actors and singers pimp their clients to children and the young.

It is critically important for totalitarian rule to "capture" or "kidnap" the child's mind with a hero. The child unquestioningly assumes a system of values and a particular ideology through heroes. As adults we often continue the allegiances we had as children.

VII.

Heroes limit the vision of man. They are like military uniforms. Young people (and sometimes old) try to be like them. Imitate them. We read all the books that our heroes have read. We wear the same clothes that our heroes have worn. We imitate the way they speak. We drink, or not drink, the same way. Heroes take all the freedom out of a man. They dictate to us. They castrate our infinite potential for creativity. A free man can have no heroes, for a hero implies the status quo. It implies a model to be emulated.

The yearning to create a hero is the totalitarian tendency

that we all have to subjugate ourselves willingly to a powerful figure. The need for a hero comes from our insecurity in ourselves. Whether in opposition or in power, whether fishing or at work, we look to "another" (anything from an esteemed colleague to god as a hero) for a cue as to what to do, when and how.

An American socialist leader at a convention of workers once said, "I can lead you through the gates of socialism, BUT someone else can just as easily lead you out." Heroes lead by crippling us. A totalitarian society cannot exist without heroes, without models. A free society cannot exist with heroes.

November 7, 1986, Marburg

INFORMANIA

VII

The Math Clock, Pop Quiz Clock Design

6·2
111|1221
102,413
-102,412
√4
-8=2-x
66|198
3(π-.14)
DC
50/2 = 100/x
√64
52-x²+x=10
126|630
1/8 . 96/2

In the future everyone will be famous for fifteen minutes.
Andy Warhol

I.

Newspapers, radio and television inform us about what is happening in the world. Information is power, goes a dictum. The more information we have, the more power. A fundamental characteristic of democracy is that people have power.

Our so-called information society has a shorter memory span and knows less history than perhaps any society of previous centuries. This is not because of censorship or a major calamity like the ancient library in Alexandria burning down. Rather, we are faced with an information overflow that makes us unselective in what we hear, see or read. There is so much news that it has become a background noise in our daily lives. Just like fast food, fast sex and fast culture, fast news is also totalitarian in that it leads to a people who are desensitized and who can no longer discriminate.

With every new event we become more and more atomized, dumbfounded, paralyzed to act or to even care about the growing violence and exploitation in the New World Order. Television coverage is sometimes credited in the U.S. for having effected that country's withdrawal from Vietnam (for the first time war was brought into our living rooms and people were shocked and came out against their country's involvement). But, since then we have been exposed to so many wars, so much famine, so much violence, that it no longer has the "Vietnam effect."

II.

The printing press was the beginning of mass information, which not only standardized the information reaching people but also made it possible for rulers to determine its contents by controlling the source. Printing technology did result in more people getting more news but it also provided the means for censorship and control. The logo of the *New York Times,* for instance is, "All the news that's fit to print," not all the news, but only what they deem fit. Before printing presses news passed by word of mouth. In a way, there were as many newspapers, as many journalists, as there were people. The eyewitness accounts and reactions became the collective information of the people. News was indeed by the people for the people of the people. Media specialists and technology have facilitated the establishment's control over news and information.

The eradication of oral history and tradition has also led to a loss of historical judgment. Through oral tradition people kept their language, culture and history alive for centuries. Today, we decide on and evaluate news only in the context of its immediate surroundings. The setting is so psychologically immediate that we do not even evaluate a military coup in one country in the context of the world order of things or what had happened in that country only even a week before. Rather, the news about the coup is perceived in the immediate context of the news items preceding it and the advert following it.

This is quite the opposite from societies in which there is crude censorship. There, the people, being hungry for news, not only savour the news item but incorporate it within a historical and political framework. In crude totalitarian societies an informed population is a danger to the viability of the government. In refined totalitarian societies on the other hand, a population that thinks it is informed is a must for the continuity of the power structure.

III.

The information–abundant society of refined totalitarianism is a history–eradicating society. It is as if everything is written on ice. It is almost impossible to have a retrospective thought, for the source will have quickly disappeared. The information is always here and now. We have little or no chance to compare it with "then" and "before."

We get the immediate news. Immediately thereafter the opinion polls give our immediate reaction to the immediate news. Thus, we are informed of what we think without having had much chance of even a discussion with neighbours, with colleagues at the workplace or even at home.

Discrimination is an active process. The passivity that comes from just attending the news rather than discriminating leads us to be easily ruled and manipulated. The refined totalitarian societies have discovered that what works for children is also valid for adults. What is new and fast will always arouse our attention and in emphasizing the present, eradicate the past. A society with little or no sense of history is easy to govern. Such a society is uncritical and easily led by the establishment.

IV.

The methods of manipulating the people through "news technology" are well known to those in the profession. Whether to present a news item with or without a photograph, the use of particular adjectives, the order of the news, the length devoted to each item, all effect the way we perceive the news. There are no measures to protect the people from these methods of manipulation.

These methods are not a secret. However, even if we were to be told about these methods of manipulation, in all likelihood, it would not be differentiated from all other information given just as quickly.

The only people who indeed "need" the news so frequently are those who follow the daily fluctuations of the market and the news in terms of influence on their holdings. For the speculators who trade their dollars for gold and their gold for wheat and their wheat for municipal bonds on the various world exchanges, each new bit of news is important, and the quicker the better.

Governments on the other hand, collect their news through their diplomats and intelligence services. It is sometimes months, sometimes years and sometimes never that the "real" news ever reaches us through the media. Governments are based on secrecy. Things are decided behind closed doors. These is no end to conspiracy theories because so much is kept from us. Where there's smoke there is fire.

News information is also becoming more visual and auditory rather than written. With the advent of the electronic newspaper it is likely that the printed newspaper, as a vehicle of current news, will disappear.

V.

We are forever discussing the affairs of the day as they are brought before us by the media. Day in and day out we attach historical importance to fleeting issues. We deem it our civic responsibility to discuss, argue and judge issues with serious concern. To this end family relationships jeopardized, communities are divided and violence may even ensue. Yet, these daily events of so-called historical significance which we find out years later to be only a tip of the iceberg or yet another example of misinformation, distortion and public opinion manipulation are soon forgotten, only to be replaced by even newer issues of "importance."

By exaggerating the day we imprison ourselves in its news while endowing ourselves with a sense of power. We are selfish. We worship our daily actions. By letting ourselves think that we are in grasp of the day, we feel that we may be influencing and even controlling history. We could, possibly have greater understanding and control of our day were we to stop attending the media altogether and begin to follow a daily newspaper from a hundred years ago, thus allowing us a sense of historical perspective.

Writing, recording and reflecting on what we have written breaks our bondage from the overflow of information. Keeping diaries, journals and video accounts of private events and thoughts gives us an opportunity to reflect on what is happening and also passes on to the following generations and historians an account of the people and times by the people themselves. We are the truth. Let them play their media games. The greatest fear of those who rule is not the opposition but not to be taken seriously.

December 2, 1986, Marburg

WHAT'S YOUR SEX?
VIII

Aurora Consurgens, Anonymos, XIV Century
symbol for the unity of opposites in alchemy

And God covered man with sleep and he slept; and he took one of his ribs and covered it with flesh; and God took one of the ribs and made a woman and he took her to the man.
Old Testament

I.

Our sex is more in the mind than in the body. Sexual roles, sexual personalities have little to do with genetically determined sexual characteristics. With the main exception of pregnancy, our sexual identities are a state of our minds. Our sexual identities are enslaved by our minds.

Let's take clothing. There is in all cultures an expectation of what men and women should wear. Ever since we began to cover ourselves for reasons not necessarily having much to do with adaptability to the environment, our sexual role and identity has been very much reflected in our clothing. Whether the phallus or the female breasts are exaggeratedly obvious as in 18th century Europe, or as inconspicuous as possible, as in Arab clothing, all effect our perception of ourselves and the opposite/other sex. Given the specific culture, men and women all dress, walk, speak, hold their cigarettes, cross their legs in ways characteristic of the particular sexual standard for their sex. The same holds for all sub-cultures.

The result is a uniform society. We, men and women, also

wear our sexual roles like strictly defined clothing. We have both our and each other's roles down perfectly. We know what to do and what to expect.

II.

The first "role," that is the first uniform that we wear in our lives is that of our sexual identity. In many societies babies are immediately differentiated from each other by the colour of their clothing (pink for girls, blue for boys). Why? Also, the adult behaves toward the boy as a male and toward the girl as a female—not only as a baby. As they mature, the children first differentiate themselves from adults and then from each other on the basis of gender. That differentiation is carried on until the end of our lives. It is the first of many uniforms that we will wear. Some are transitional uniforms and, like being a teenager, will be worn and taken off. Nationality uniforms can also be exchanged across generations, as for instance, in the case of Europeans who have become Americans. The sexual uniform is not only the first, but it is also never taken off, except in rare cases of sex change operations.

From the behaviorist psychologist's point of view, our sexual role is the role in which we are most conditioned. It is the role which is most reinforced by others as well as by ourselves.

It is important to emphasize that the sexual role is basically learned. Which particular role is learned is based on which role is taught. With all of us having a combination of the male hormone androgen and the female hormone estrogen, we biologically have a great deal more in common with the other sex than our rigid sexualities allow. In a sense we are not sexually diametrically opposed to each other. The term, "the opposite sex" is not particularly apt.

An infinite variety of sexual roles are possible. Anthropology shows us the many different roles that have been assumed by the male and female. What is important to note however, is that the roles have always been mutually exclusive. The female and the male roles have been clearly defined against each other. The "correct" formation/socialization of sexual identity leads to harnessing the freedom of the child. The child, in his trusting love, allows himself to be harnessed. The child, in his physical dependence, has no other choice but to be harnessed.

Throughout life we continue to harness ourselves and each other in sexual roles.

III.

Psychologists speak of the importance of a healthy sexual identity. That is, a male should think of himself in association with all behaviours, personality characteristics and physical attributes as a male and the female as a female. The difference should be as clear as night and day. Any ambiguity, cross over, say the psychologists, can result in very important problems of adjustment.

Yet it is the totalitarian nature of sexual identity that causes many of us to have psychological problems. Because our own particular image of ourselves may not be in keeping with the image that our father, family, school, priest, peers, police, president have of how a boy/man/girl/woman should behave, we are reprimanded not to be like "that," and encouraged to be like "this." In trying to fit that image, in trying to live up to a particular standard sexual identity, in trying to wear clothes not made specifically for us, we all have problems. The problem, of course, is not because we are the way we are or think the way we think. The problem comes from trying to become like that which we are not. The source of the problem is the so-called adjustment required from us to conform to the totalitarian standards, to wear the uniform of accepted identities. In trying to please the establishment we become alienated from our own selves. The more we adjust, the more totalitarian we become ourselves. At the end of the adjustment process, we also begin to demand that others adjust. The process of adjustment is further marked by developing fears and double standards. It is out of fear that we may not please those holding either the carrot or the stick, that we try to adjust. If the voice of the self, if our own drummer, can still be faintly heard in spite of this adjustment process, we develop double standards leading to a discrepancy between the way we want to be and the way we show ourselves. Throughout all this, the establishment figures are ambivalent—they are loved, needed and feared at the same time.

In the course of our lives, we only share (even than not fully), our multi-faceted sexuality in the secluded secret, private love that we have in adulthood with that rare person whom we trust. But, not only does that happen infrequently, but also much too late. Even with that rare person, it is not easy to liberate that, which has for much of our lifetime, been suppressed with our collaboration.

The oppressive power of sexual identity is felt most in closed communities. A woman, "a bit on the masculine side," or a man, "a bit on the feminine side," cannot exist in such closed societies. Our use of language further reflects the totalitarianism of sexual identity. The existence of such pejorative words as effeminate, emasculate, butch, queer, and the connotations of hundreds of other words referring to deviations from the standard sex model are examples. Any societal norm of a healthy sexual identity is a means of oppression. Furthermore, to the degree that normalcy is totalitarian, it is also pathological.

IV.

That a male has to act like a male and the female as a female subjugates both sexes to uniform standards which have no particular biological function for the maintenance of the species. It serves however a very particular function for the maintenance of order.

Power depends on and demands obedience. Marching left foot first has nothing to do with winning wars. Yet, it conditions soldiers to obey unquestioningly. And soldiers go unquestioningly to their death. Societal order, established through enforcing simple and arbitrary standards, as in the case of our sexual behaviour, gives freedom—in the sense of the establishment interfering as little in the life of the individual as possible—little chance to develop. Sexual identity models are artificial constructs built by the dominant forces in society and maintained as long as they serve their purpose. It is more or less an unstated but always present standard. We have such strict sexual standards that any deviation is immediately noticed. The maintenance of strict sexual roles gives order to society. Uniformity and standardization are ever–present reminders of the presence of an authority. The authority is all the more powerful, something akin to the power of a god, because the sexual standards are not written. Thus, one always has to be on one's guard. Officials have been forced to resign in many countries because of what are called "sexual scandals." No law has been broken. No written agreement has been violated. The unexpected sexual behaviour however (for example a politician having had sexual intercourse with a prostitute) is enough of a reason for an immediate resignation and its acceptance. Yet no government in history has ever fallen from power because there was prostitution in that country. Sexual standards are only individually oppressive.

Going against unwritten sexual standards is as critical as being suspected of associating with traitors. Thus many a government official has been known to resign because of contacts with agents without their realization. Being even close to a traitor and breaking a sexual standard are considered almost equally grave transgressions against society. The person often immediately removes himself (through resigning, escaping, suicide) even before the establishment has a chance to ostracize him.

It is "understandable" that a society should try to keep in check murderers, drug pushers, traffic violators—but why those who do not dress or behave within the image of the particular sexual identity? Power is most oppressive when it is arbitrary. The enforcement of sexual identity is one of the most oppressive uses of power. Yet, and unquestioningly, we give this oppressive power to the state.

V.

Sex related roles, clothing, mores, standards are one of the main sources of power, one of the main points of legitimation for any regime. We, due to our strong obedience to our gender roles, give carte blanche power to regimes to enforce an understanding of a sexual code.

Although there are checks in almost any regime to protect the individual from the state, there are no measures against the use of totalitarian models to enforce gender roles upon all individuals.

We take it for granted that the accepted behaviour and image of the female and the male are imposed upon us in almost all messages and images of society. The non-accepted is only legitimately seen in art or pathology. It is hardly taken notice of by society however, since art appeals to an elite and the "pathology" takes place either in the private offices of psychologists and psychiatrists or in the wards of mental hospitals.

The family, the educational system and religion all reinforce the totalitarian mutually exclusive male-female roles. All three institutions have very clear-cut and often the same ideas as to what is "male" and what is "female." Although history abounds with instances of disagreements amongst the three institutions with respect to various economical, political and cultural issues, they are united in their perception of sexual roles. They are united in enforcing the same absolute sexual standards.

Even nature is not as restricted in its biological sex roles as we are accustomed to think. I remember a fish in the London Aquarium. Something that looked a bit like a seahorse. In the description below the tank it was written that one male fish is usually accompanied by five or six females—each with a particular rank, from the most senior and favoured down to the lowest. When the male dies the number one female changes sex and becomes the male—the leader of the school. The previously number two female is now most favoured lady-fish of the new male.

Nature allows for infinite possibilities in terms of biological differences and inter and intra-species variations. We also have infinite possibilities in terms of our psychological potential for variation and freedom. Yet, as if it is not enough to dominate and destroy the other species and eventually perhaps our own species with them, in our totalitarian order, we also block our potential for infinite sexual expression. The human, having a mind and imagination, does not need the ordering and the restrictions of biology to limit or enhance his identity. We have infinite possibilities because we are curious by nature and can imagine. To realize such possibilities there must be a liberation from sexual identity.

VI.

"Women's Liberation," an ethnocenthric (sexocentric) term takes up only one side of the issue—the subjugated role of the female. As long as the aims of liberation are defined with respect to sexual identity, as long as liberation is looked upon in reference to and equality with the male, there can be no liberation.

Often, the oppressed yearn to become like their oppressors. The once oppressed also become first rate oppressors. History is full of such examples from the young African republics that replaced colonialist rule to Jewish prisoners in concentration camps who voluntarily took over the duties of the guards. Though a reordering of the world in which both male and female identities evolve toward sharing on new terms is espoused by feminism, sexual identities are still defined against one another rather than individually. What has never been on the agenda is the shedding of all uniforms.

An important step toward freedom is the liberation of the human from sexual identity, either as male or female. "Look at me as a person not as a sexual object," is a statement of revolt against the existing order. It however denies the existence of sex and carries seeds of yet a greater totalitarianism. Our technological innovations along with notions of sexual egalitarianism are taking us toward the denial of evolution based male and female potentialities.

The current mechanistic biological view suggests that all sexual differences begin and end in copulation and pregnancy. Other than that there should be complete equality—equality meaning that one should pay as little attention as possible to one's or the other's sex. And now, a society is in the offing in which even copulation and pregnancy will not be necessary for the continuation of the species. Artificial insemination, test tube babies, genetical engineering and eventually a totally artificial growth environment for the embryo will make this sexless society even more possible.

A sexless society is more totalitarian and uniform than a society based on two sexes with one sex dominating the other. With the ominous threat of a sexless society, freedom is protecting sexual differentiation, even if it may include male or female chauvinists.

VII.

Sexual identity is not a dichotomous, mutually exclusive choice between being a male or a female. Nor is it a continuum along a scale with femaleness and maleness at opposite poles. It is also not bisexuality either which might yet be another category for a uniform. It is an individually created understanding and reflection of one's sex—like an ever changing tune hummed by us, or a floral garden that continually changes it's colour, form and smell combinations. Thus, in that sense, each individual has a different sex, since each individual will make up his own combination and permutation of all possible behaviours and imaginations with respect to one's identity. No longer would one wear a sexual uniform easily recognized by oneself and others.

The eradication of sexually determined roles will enhance the individuality, enrich the personality of the human. It will increase our repertoire for behaviour and personality to unthought variations. Furthermore such a liberation will mean an end to our submissiveness, to the roles already determined for us by existing standards. It is only on the basis of such standards that the establishment finds excuses to rule and oppress.

An ever-changing identity is a function of independence and trust. Liberation from sexual identity is not to have one.

November 11, 1986, Marburg

FREEDOM FROM CHOICE
IX

Kuan Yin with 11 heads, VIII century
Tang dynasty

We all live in a yellow submarine, a yellow submarine,
a yellow submarine.
The Beatles

I.

For many centuries we wondered about the existence of a free will. The preoccupation of present times is with freedom of choice. The focus has shifted from questioning the meaning to emphasizing the action. We look upon restraints on choosing as infringements of freedom. Most of us profess that democracy is about choice and totalitarianism a lack of it. The right to choose and what is chosen are very important to us. It is an extension of our personality, a part of our identity.

In a universe of change and uncertainty however, all choice is an act of pretension. In choosing we lose any chance of contemplating or comprehending the whole. In choosing we take up sides and oppress those by us to stay with us, fight those against us to be with us, and condemn to oblivion those who do not choose. Choosing is a self-imposed order of divide and rule. By choosing and taking sides we divide both knowledge and people. In dividing we rule over bits of knowledge which become dogma and a collection of people which become an unquestioning crowd.

In choosing we become right, righteous and damning. In choosing a side, any side, we become totalitarian.

II.

We are tempted to choose. We who control less and less of what goes on in our daily lives and the world, we who have become increasingly aware of our insignificance since Hiroshima and the possibility of a nuclear holocaust, derive a false sense of strength from choosing. It is a veil over our eyes through which we see ourselves as controllers of a system that oppresses us. As there are those who eat and become obese to feel psychologically secure, we too, consume one choice after another. In our collective insecurity, we tend through choice and consumption, toward material and psychological obesity. Never have a people chosen so much and assessed themselves and others in terms of what they have chosen as we in this century.

Choosing is an act reinforced over and over in our daily consumption of material goods. Most of our choices in life are what we purchase in a shopping centre. A North American probably makes more choices in a shopping centre in an hour than an Asian peasant makes in his lifetime. The conditioned consumer-oriented choice behaviour is generalized and repeats itself in other situations ranging from culture and politics to friendship and marriage. Rather than living processes we consume choices.

The relatively unrestricted act of choosing as a consumer takes away whatever significance and sanctity there may be in "choice" itself. The American poet Robert Frost's contemplation on "The Road Not Taken" is indeed from a past time. Choice has become insignificant in that very system—democracy—that is purportedly built on it. The most typical, the most frequent choose behaviour is that which leads to the ownership of what has been chosen. We are conditioned to choosing things that we end up owning. In owning we become powerful. Both the act of buying and the state of ownership endow one with power. The relationship between the owner and the object owned exists independently of the intrinsic, inherent value of the object.

The act of choosing is accompanied by a feeling of mastering, of being the master over the process, of being the master over that which one chooses. It is a feeling of power. It is an, "I have chosen..." feeling not requiring any reciprocity. The relationship is complete in spite of the fact that it is one-sided. "I," who have chosen, do not have to be chosen in return for the relationship to be complete. I need not be accepted. I cannot be challenged in turn by what I side with or against. I can choose a President and call Jesus my prophet. I can reject all the mighty and great who walk and have walked on earth and feel stronger than all of them put together. The psychological act of choosing to be for or against makes us the supreme judge. No one can challenge us.

Like consumer preferences, all types of allegiances are also the result of one-sided relationships. They are simply chosen. The one-sided choice is the most complete power relationship. It is the ultimate in domination. But it is also a fantasy. For although our choice and support is wooed by political parties, sellers of consumer goods, entertainers and religious sects, it is actually they who control us by offering, limiting and defining our choices. In deciding to choose we assign rulers. It is they who amass fortune and power through our support.

That which has been chosen in this one-sided relationship never refuses our support. The relationship between the anonymous individual and the established institution is non- discriminating. No political party refuses a vote, no religion a disciple, no club a fan, no company a customer, no producer a consumer. Just the opposite, we are exploited for our inclination to choose and commit ourselves to our choice.

III.

Choosing may also be simply unhealthy. Especially if the choice is difficult it can lead to mental stress and physical illness. Some ulcers, which result from exactly that, can be fatal. Many neuroses as well are exacerbated by states of indecision. Though the magnitude of stress to bring about such illnesses varies individually, there is no doubt that we are all subject to it. The situation also does not end once a decision is made. Many of us wonder if we've made the right choice and therefore reconsider. That dilemma triggers yet another stress since we are also taught that it is bad to change sides and that a strong person sticks to his decision. There are also many instances where we stick by our choice in spite of resentment, simply to avoid yet another stress.

All this, because we are taught that one's future, happiness, wealth and power are all critically influenced by decision and choice, by being on the right side. Most of us end up being members of a side without even having chosen it. Rather, we assume identities which we rationalize as being choices. Like our names that come "attached" to us at birth, such things as religion, ideology, nationality, affiliation with a sports team also become attached to us as a function of our family and the social and physical environment in which we grow up. It is not a psychologically innate mechanism in us that we choose one side over another or choose any side at all. It is rather an unquestioning inclination to the social structures that we are born into and grow up in. Choice and choosing sides is a part of society's way of life but it is also detrimental to one's health, happiness and an understanding of life. To be with an idea, person or a thing need not mean that one is either for or against it. It need not necessitate that we end up on opposing sides. While we make no conscious attempt to join sides however, the sides are engaged in an endeavour to exist and be strong and seek supporters. To this end they have missionaries, hire public relations personnel and even make war, with us as the soldiers.

Choosing sides prevents one from expanding, experiencing, communicating. In choosing sides we construct ghettoes into which we commit ourselves with zeal. The other person is on the wrong side. He is not like us. We are superior. They are inferior. Things having to do with our side, we know by role learning. We repeat our beliefs, arguments, assets day in and day out like an unchanging chant. Doubt is bad for the morale. It is against team spirit. Any doubt, questions our belonging and leads us to a feeling of being lost. Choosing is belonging. In our belonging we have friends. Otherwise we are outcasts.

It is in choosing and belonging however that we also lose sight of ourselves and any sense of perspective. In belonging we lose our capacity to make self-portraits. We become so immersed in what we have chosen that any distinction between "I" the individual and "we" who belong, becomes less and less clear. Furthermore, the "I" and that which has been chosen also become enmeshed with each other. Any identification with the chosen object or side also changes its perception. Each choice changes one's self-perception as well as the perception of the object.

IV.

The process of the socialization of the individual is tantamount to the withering away of freedom. Socialization is a function of societal structures and definitions of relationships. The society, the structure, is confirmed by the individual through choice.

From infancy on, the individual is constantly put before choices. We are asked to choose and in choosing we become slaves. In choosing we lose our freedom.

We begin to lose our freedom by being forced to make choices amongst/between things over which no choice can be made. We are forced to choose amongst things that cannot be divided or excluded from each other.

One of the most radical forced choices a child faces is about love. Love is neither quantifiable nor mutually exclusive. One cannot love "so much" or "this much." Nor does loving "this" exclude loving "that." The totalitarianism of being forced to choose and quantify with respect to love, puts love in the context of a hierarchical power relationship. It is no longer a free, all embracing feeling. It can no longer be altruistic.

The parents are usually the first to confront the child with totalitarian choice. Sometimes together, sometimes in secret from each other, they ask the child, "Who do you love most Daddy or Mommy?" If they don't ask, they look for small tell tale signs in the behaviour of the child. The, "Who do you love most?" question is transferred and generalized by the siblings. Now, the child also mentally assumes the hierarchical structure, wondering which one of his brothers or sisters the parents love the most. Another favourite question the parents put before children is,"How much do you love me?"or, "Show me how much you love me." Thus, in the very early years, the individual is introduced to a hierarchical ordering of love.

It is soon "discovered" that through giving and withholding love one can also control the behaviour of others, especially those close. In fact, withholding love is an often a recommended psychological method of obtaining discipline in a child. Thus, love becomes an instrument of control. The "love choice" is like the original sin of totalitarianism. From then on, one choice follows another. We choose our best friend. Over the years we choose many more and keep on replacing one best friend with yet another. There are also always those we dislike the most. Thus, there is always someone on top, the best friend, and someone at the bottom, the most disliked. We also learn to choose from our toys favouring one over the other and from our dolls which are also ranked in a rigid hierarchical order.

Then comes gender. Though we are given our sex genetically we are also made to choose it psychologically. The psychological identification is again totalitarian, for it is an affirmation of one sex and a condemnation of the other. Boys and girls both look down upon, exclude each other. They choose not to choose each other. They learn to choose not to be with each other. They learn to typecast each other. All this, according to textbooks, is a normal part of growing up in the socialization process. The genetic differences become exaggerated within a psychological field. They take on a new perception with the differences again being used as psychological weapons in a power structure. The choice leads to totalitarianism, this time based on sexual differences. Such differences would not lead to totalitarianism were they perceived in terms of contributing to the greater whole and unity rather than being mutually exclusive categories.

At about the age of six, children begin to play games together. A game is a form of play, a form of amusement, something we do to have a good time, to enjoy ourselves. Yet, simultaneously with learning games, children also learn to choose sides. The most popular games are those in which there are sides. There are instances where children concentrate more on choosing sides than playing the game. It might even be said that the game exists so that sides may be chosen. Who chose whom is a very dramatic event in a child's life.

Such choices lead to fights, jealousy, frustration, aggression, compromising behaviour, pity. All these games of choosing sides are also a part of the socializing process of the child. Even before adulthood, the child is very much a part and agent of the totalitarian society. As an adult, only the subject matter of the games changes; the "we against them" paradigm continues through classes, nation states, religions.

The historical evolution of children's games suggests that even across centuries they have not changed all that much. The concept of including some and excluding others has been a part of games, whether society is feudal, capitalist or socialist. In all cases the totalitarian structure in children's games is there. Such games are a reflection of societal structure. Any society in which those who want to belong can be excluded through the choice of others represses its members. Choosing sides is also a form of mutual ostracism. It is based on some notion of superiority/inferiority, always a reflection of the order of power.

Thus, all the psychological weapons are already installed in the mind/paradigm of the child. Discrimination on the basis of race, social class, intelligence are all based on the set of perceptive structures built upon the basis of forced choice, mutual exclusiveness, quantification and comparison.

V.

The westernized and so called pluralistic contemporary society, in its daily life, has become perhaps one of the most segregated of all societies. First, people have become segregated from each other according to age. The elderly are by themselves in their own ghettoes (homes for the elderly, retirement communities etc.), the young are forever organized to be together during and after school, the middle-aged everywhere else. People are also segregated according to their income, race, religion and affinity to the establishment. There are fewer and fewer communities in which different races, professions, income groups and ages live in the same neighbourhood. Contemporary society, in the way we live, is very much the image of a totalitarian corporate society. The establishment deals with and manipulates people as sociological categories.

We, as people, stay in those categories into which we have divided ourselves. The young want to be with the young, the blacks with the blacks, the artists with the artists, the feminists with the feminists, the soldiers with the soldiers. Our way of life is segregated and totalitarian with each group seeking its own interests and identity.

Alternative movements, those who refuse the ways of the establishment, also choose the same totalitarian model. They live in specific neighbourhoods, have their own restaurants, particular way of dressing and speaking and even vacation spots. They also choose to be segregated and are closed to outsiders. What appears at first to be an attempt at liberalization is another instance of segregation. Although they cry for freedom against the establishment, they are oppressive to their own members. The oppression and the monotony come from the self-imposed totalitarian order.

We choose to seek those who are like us. Those unlike us, disturb us. Not only do we not want them to, but we also don't even know how to communicate with them. Yet, togetherness in our own flock is a monotonous reinforcement of sameness, a repetition of an endless vigil. We impose an order of oneness. We want everyone to think and behave in the same way. Those who show any individuality, uniqueness are not tolerated. We are bored yet we submit to the group. We dare not cross borders that we yearn to cross. We put up the very borders that we dare not cross.

VI.

By choosing "this" over "that" we block all paths to liberation. The forced choice paradigm leads one to think in terms of "more" or "less" with inequality becoming an imminent part of our thinking and appraisal. In this sense we replicate the material basis of inequality in concepts and evaluations. That which cannot be perceived in terms of equality, that which cannot be measured and compared, become objects of equalization in the name of equality and democracy.

There would be no sides in a society which upholds the individual and reinforces the utmost variation in biological/psychological characteristics. Solutions to injustices in society are determined and limited by our socialization experience. Due to our habit of quantifying and comparing, we seek, as a democratic solution, to equalize.

The aim to achieve equality leads to cancelling all difference, and ends up as just another form of totalitarianism and the standardization of man. Sexual equality, for instance, cannot be obtained at the cost of eradicating sexual differences. Technology, when used to make women more like men in the name of "liberation" from archaic mammalian characteristics, can only lead to a singularly cheerless, standard type of human. Political equality as well cannot be obtained through the choice paradigm. The totalitarianism of choice can neither be eradicated through minimizing choice —as in a single "choice" society—the most crude from of totalitarianism or by increasing choice, as in the "multi-choice" structured society, which is the most refined type.

It is the concept of choice in and of itself that is totalitarian. Intelligence, beauty, love, justice, freedom cannot be measured or compared. They can only exist to the degree that they are not defined or standardized. Any attempt at even a definition is a violation of the concept. Once defined, intelligence becomes dull, beauty uninspiring, love is consumed, justice needs justification and freedom simply ceases to exist outside of its defined form.

VII.

It is a sign of the totalitarianism in us that we are engaged in a process of choosing mutually exclusive categories to which we then profess our belonging. We seem to act in accordance with a "Principle of Constant Change and Immediate Belonging."

We are always changing. Many of our ideas, attitudes, behaviours change over the years. In all these changes, rather than recognizing the process of change, rather than seeing how we are different at each stage after each experience, rather than seeing our contradictions, we look at things always from our present position, not at all conscious of the changes in us that have taken and will take place. For example, in terms of the chronological stages of life and the personality changes that are associated with them, we always choose attitudes and behaviours of that particular stage we happen to be in, deeming it superior to all other stages. Thus, the middle-aged say they have to control the younger generations and put up with the elderly. The young do not trust or believe in anybody old. The old look with fear at the young who are destroying the world.

We always have in our minds a sense of what is right and what is wrong. That sense, of course, is relative and always changes not only as a function of the person's age and experiences but also as a function of economic, social and political changes. Yet at each point, in reference to our particular opinion at that point, we always or almost always see our position as being the correct one against all other positions. Rather than seeing contradictions and the process of change, we deal with the momentary as a permanent truth and reality. We judge (in our favour) between generations, across cultures, against classes in numerous everyday situations. Throughout our lives we belong to many sides—some short lived, some lasting a lifetime.

One typically humorous example of the Principle of Constant Change and Immediate Belonging that is short-lived is to be found in the behaviour of passengers on crowded Istanbul public buses. After entering the bus from the front door, one immediately begins to push one's way toward the already crowded back, as there are others right behind who are getting on the bus. Those in the front shout toward the back, "Hey, you in the back, get a move on, there's plenty of space." Those in the back protest at being pushed. After a few stops, those in the front have made it to the back. Now they can be heard shouting, "Hey, you in front stop pushing, we can't breathe." In a matter of minutes the person who identifies himself with those in the front changes sides and identifies himself with those in the back—constant change and immediate belonging.

A longer term example given by the American sociologist Vance Packard is about changes in the eating habits of Italian-Americans as they move up in society. At first, the poor immigrant Italians eat spaghetti. The next generation "moves up" to hamburgers. They would not be caught dead eating Italian food. Next on the hierarchy is steak. None of that cheap American working class food. Then comes European cuisine and especially French food, which they once considered the fare for effete snobs. At the top of the pinnacle, when they've reached the upper class, they invite their guests over for a special evening of Italian spaghetti, in which they take great pride. Constant Change, Immediate Belonging.

Not only is there no empathy for the other group to which they once belonged, but the other groups are also looked upon as threatening, inferior, strange. Our affirmative choice also implies a condemnation of others, in spite of the fact that we may have been "that other" at another time and place.

VIII.

Psychological experiments clearly demonstrate how choice not only alters our perception of reality but also makes us pawns in totalitarian structures that arise as a result of our identification with a particular choice.

A concept called cognitive dissonance says that if we have made a choice that disagrees with our previous outlook, we will change our attitude to be in keeping with the present choice. More clearly put, a choice is always justified by changing the past, by rewriting history. In spite of past experience the present choice rules the past. If we make a choice that is not in keeping with our past belief, experience or behaviour, we tend to reorder the past rather than change our choice.

Empirical evidence from psychological experiments seems to clearly show that making a decision produces dissonance—a psychologically upsetting state which we need to put at rest. Observations show for instance that people in the market for a new car read ads for many kinds of autos. Once they have purchased a car, they only read ads for the car they own, avoiding ads for other makes—a very clear example of the totalitarianism of choosing sides. With each side that we choose, we close ourselves to alternatives. An experiment was made with children who were tempted to cheat in order to win prizes. The children who cheated developed more lenient attitudes toward cheating. Those who resisted showed harsher attitudes than before.

Another experiment, also from the U.S., shows dramatically how from initially equal college students, two very distinct groups can emerge as a result of being placed in different sides. In this experiment by Zimbardo, college students reached through an ad soliciting volunteers for an experiment on prison life were randomly placed in two groups—guards and prisoners. They were placed in a simulated prison and the prisoners were asked to obey the rules of the prison (lights out times, not damaging prison property, etc.) and the guards to enforce them. The experiment had to be stopped after just six days because while the guards became bullies, the prisoners behaved in ways that actually helped to justify the dehumanizing treatment at the hands of the guards. According to Zimbardo, "in less than a week, the experience of prison undid (temporarily) a life-time of learning—human values were suspended, self-concepts were challenged and the ugliest most base pathological side of human nature surfaced." Yet another example of Constant Change and Immediate Belonging.

IX.

We feel that it is not only our duty but also our right to choose a side. The freedom to choose is looked upon as one of the pillars of democracy. We rarely stop to think that our choices are usually chosen by others and that we can only select from what has been put before us.

This is true for practically everything we encounter in daily life, including consumption items, politics and culture. Choosing sides reinforces the totalitarianism of what has been given from above. It gives legitimacy to the particular system. We select sides on the basis of the societal order of the time. We choose sides on the basis of the commonly accepted blueprint of society. The order of society compels us to choose sides. In the Byzantine Empire, one was either a Blue or a Green, in the USA today, either a Democrat or a Republican, in the Soviet Union of yesteryear, a communist. Other positions are considered odd, heretical, strange. Were no sides to be chosen, the reigning hierarchical totalitarian order would be challenged. It would face collapse. Not choosing sides is a challenge to the legitimacy of the established order.

Calling for an end to beauty contests for example, jeopardizes male domination. The male domination-exploitation is so self-evident that we have not a "women's beauty contest" but simply a "beauty contest". Each beauty contest held and choice of a winner reinforces the subjugated role of women and a hierarchical quantitative measure of beauty. No beauty contests, is not only an end to one aspect of exploitation but it also liberates "beauty" from being subject to a standard totalitarian measure.

The same applies in a much wider sense to the various political systems.

In many Western countries there is little difference between the policy of the major parties when they become the government. In fact there is a problem, especially in the U.S., to try to show the people that the two parties are indeed different. Image making, the use of advertising companies and psychologists are vitally important in elections, as parties and candidates seek a difference that is no longer there. In many countries fewer voters are participating in elections so that even popularly elected persons are chosen by a minority. In terms of numbers, the elections have long lost their legitimacy. The majority of multi-party system democracies are run by minority governments or presidents. However, our preoccupation on the contest between "this" and "that," still reinforces the legitimacy of the particular rulers.

One often points to the freedom of association in the West as an example of democracy based on the pluralism of choice. We see hundreds and hundreds of action groups, associations, clubs, cults and religious sects espousing various causes and movements. However, they are also part of the consumption paradigm ever changing in current times. Especially in our youth, many of us drift from one group to another. Very rarely do the efforts of these organizations or movements lead to any structural change. By taking up such causes, usually as proxies, in the name of those directly suffering the injustice, we also subject ourselves to certain restraints that give structure to and limit our life experiences. Organizations that we form in the name of freedom for others often end up limiting our ability to see the limits of our own freedom. It prevents us from taking up issues that we face in our everyday lives. Many compensate for their alienation and political powerlessness in their own milieu by taking up humanitarian issues on behalf of others in especially the so-called Third World countries.

Rulers have no qualms about those who might be of potential danger to the system and who instead choose to concentrate their efforts as proxies rather than questioning the oppression and exploitation experienced first-hand. Political action is thus consumed rather than effecting fundamental change.

Whether we participate or not, knowing that people have

chosen, knowing that someone has been chosen, reinforces in us the belief that it is through choice that the ruling establishment exists. We have come to such a point that the rulers no longer have to justify their existence to us. We justify their existence ourselves. No longer do we have kings who present themselves as representatives of God on earth. That masquerade is over. There's no need, as there was in the past, for the rulers to fool us. By playing the game, we do that perfectly well ourselves. All rulers have to do is to keep on periodically saying that they are the servants of the people, that they represent the will of the people. As before, we still have absolute rulers. What is different is that they receive their legitimacy from us rather than a god. What is more significant however, is not how we get rulers, but that we still have the "rulers" and the "ruled".

X.

One guarantee of a democracy, it is said, is the opportunity for groups to organize and pursue their interests. How else could the workers in the West have won, protected and advanced their rights for a forty hour week, sickness and vacation benefits and the right to strike, had they not formed unions to oppose the capitalists? Is there not the historically and the ethically compelling argument that one must choose the side of the exploited against the exploiters? Yes, but not at the expense of sacrificing the principle to the expediently available gain.

The workers of the world are not united in practice or in theory. Their particular interests can even be diametrically opposed. The gains of workers in one place are sometimes the cause of losses to workers in another. The rights of the working class in the West were built not simply on the basis of their struggle but on the wealth obtained from the exploitation of millions of other workers under colonialism. Today, the First World and "international" cities continue to become richer at the expense of the Third World and the periphery. Within the Third World, the gains of the organized industrial workers are often at the expense of the individual unorganized peasants.

For over a century public opinion has backed the cause of the workers, their unions and parties over capitalists and employers. We have chosen the side of the worker. However not all work done by workers benefits the world or its people. In praising the worker as opposed to the mighty rulers, Bertold Brecht in a poem asks who built Thebes and the pyramids. He neglects to ask who built the bombs that destroyed Hiroshima and Nagasaki. The rulers, certainly, but not without the workers. The glorified side that we have chosen, the workers, has not once protested, handed out leaflets, or gone out on strike to protest their own participation in making guns, tanks and missiles. Sons and daughters are killed by the weapons made by their fathers and mothers. The workers strike for higher wages and less working hours. They do not strike against their role in the industry that thrives on killing people. Whether it is a worker in a socialist or capitalist country, both have worked in keeping the war business going. Not once in history has a labour union gone on strike to protest the collaboration of their workers in the arms industry. Not even for an hour. Not even for a second of silence on August 6, the day Hiroshima was bombed and the world changed forever. As usual, the side, in this case the workers, promotes only it's shortsighted interests of preserving their jobs and increasing their income.

The same can be said for workers in many other industries which pollute the environment, poison people with improper drugs, kill children through unsafe toys, make holes in the ozone layer through aerosols and sell inferior dangerous products to the Third World whose manufacture for the Western market has been made illegal. The workers of Nestle never went on strike or even issued a press statement criticizing the use of breast milk substitutes that according to UNICEF and WHO reports, lead indirectly to the death of over a million infants yearly. No workers on fishing boats protested the killing of whales and other species that are becoming extinct due to hunting. Those who daily make production possible —the employers and the workers— have never opposed each other on these issues. The points of contention have not been based on the fundamental principle of the well-being of the world and people but rather on the existence of sides and their particular interests.

With respect to universal principles there can be no sides. The peace movement of the 1980's was another example of a side based on self-interest. It was a protest movement not for peace but against war. "Don't kill us, we want to live," they said. It was not against all wars but a possible war in Europe. In the meantime wars went on throughout the world. The ten-year Iran-Iraq war is but one example. Where was the peace movement then? The movement, based on self-interest was hypocritical, it did not adhere to a universal principle of peace and harmony throughout the world.

The process of man opposing man throughout history has not brought us any nearer to freedom or happiness. It has only changed the type of exploitation and oppression.

When individuals with differences (on the basis of football club affiliation, political party, race, religion, country) come together on those rare occasions, their typical inclination is to profess their belonging to the brotherhood of man. They profess to their oneness with no or little mention of differences. When we come back with "our own kind," however, any discussion about the other is made on the basis of our belonging to our particular category. That is, we again bond on the basis of our differences from the other. Almost always we are, "We men," "We women," "We blacks," "We Muslims," "We intellectuals," "We Americans." Hardly ever, is "We" meant to denote everyone. That is, "We, all living things," "We humans," "We, the universe." Through choosing, we divide "WE" into many "we." In spite of its property as a word to be all inclusive, "we" is usually used to denote an exclusivity. We only means we when it does not mean "we."

XI.

Do all choices by necessity impose a totalitarian structure? Are there no ethical, moral choices that we must make in order to stand fast against those who violate basic freedoms and principles and lie about the truth?

The act of choosing usually leads to polarization in society. It does not facilitate understanding or harmony but rather divides people into camps. The camps in turn usually become so entrenched that the camp itself, the side itself, becomes more important than the particular issue or principle. Once the sides are established arguments, research, rationalizations are produced to justify the existence of the side. This holds even for science, in spite of the fact that, above all else, it's based on critical thought.

Yet, the history of science is full of incidents where attachment to particular views have promoted their propagation while preventing the perception of evidence to the contrary. Political and religious history also provides many examples of the above. Religious differences in the name of "God's Truth" have eventually always led to new interpretations, persecutions, new religions and religious wars. Politics, sugar-coated with utopian visions, is nothing more than seizing and holding power.

Be it science, religion or politics, however, in all fields there have been men who have sacrificed themselves on the basis of their principles. They have stood fast before opposing crowds, condemning colleagues, judges and torturers, never recanting. Persons of principle can be found in all sects, in all ideologies, in all groups. Altruism is not a distinguishing characteristic of any particular movement or school of thought. All sides have their heroes, their men of principle. It is on the basis of these altruistic, steadfast persons that all sides have a moral appeal to their supporters. It is on the basis of such people that they claim a moral, ethical superiority to other sides.

There is no ideology, no religion, no side whatsoever in our history, which has been consistent in upholding principles. We need go no further than the first of the Ten Commandments. "Thou Shalt Not Kill," which has been constantly violated, especially in the name of fighting for god's cause.

In spite of such inconsistency and hypocrisy, we are all fortunately still aware, no matter what our religious or ideological inclinations are (if any), of certain universal moral/ethical principles.

Our universal heritage of moral/ethical values has not come to us through opposition as a result of having chosen sides. The act of upholding principles through choosing sides and opposition calls forth "destructive energies" or better put the application of our energies in a destructive manner. Principles, can only be upheld by example, not force.

Choosing a side by definition implies a wish for victory

for our side and a defeat for the other. It means that the sides are struggling so that eventually one will accept the superiority of the other. No matter what the principle, should one still remain, the final act of submission and defeat results in a totalitarian relationship. Also, the longer the struggle between the sides, the more it is accepted over time, perhaps unconsciously, that the means justify the end.

Gandhi, having recognized that defeat implies a loss of face, an embarrassment, introduced in his concept of civil disobedience (*satragyana*) the opportunity for his opposition not to be defeated, but rather to join voluntarily the idea that they had been opposing. Still however, it does not do away with the destructive energies unleashed as a result of the act of opposition.

How we come to believe in the sanctity of life is not by chance. Our civilization could well have developed along the lines of cannibalism, a practice we are all capable of. Then there would have been no need to speak about the sanctity of life. However, our civilization is an accumulation of the energies of man applied creatively. Literature, music, architecture, medicine, philosophy are all dependent on certain individuals applying their energies creatively. Life is worth preserving on the basis of such creative work. It is our concept of beauty that enables us to talk about the wonders of man, the richness of man, the genius of man.

Our ode to ourselves is based on the "beauty" that we have created. Even if beauty is relative, the act of creation, the expansion of the mind and the senses, is the highest plane that man can achieve. It is because there have been so many examples of our creativity in history that we look upon life as worth preserving.

Destructive forces like the death penalty, wars or the killing off of other species cannot be eradicated through opposition. They can be overcome only by continuing to create even more, by making it possible for more and more people not only to enjoy the opportunity to taste and appreciate what has been created before, but also to encourage all to partake in the act of creation. Creation is the affirmation of life. Such affirmation shared by many is enough to lay aside any notions of man killing man. Should it still take place occasionally it will not be through consensus but as an accident, like mutations in biology.

XII.

The essence of freedom is not in choosing one object, one person, one idea, one flower over another. Freedom is not an act that leads to a hierarchical ordering or mutual exclusivity. Freedom is not an act of rejection. It is an act of embracing. "The freedom of choice" as a concept is opposed to the state of freedom. Freedom is not "either this or that" but rather an "all or nothing" act.

Freedom is one's capacity to go into depth in any particular action or idea (still without infringing upon the freedom of others). It is a reflection of our desire and ability to pursue to the nth degree. Pursue what? Whatever one wills. The exercise of freedom is an all encompassing act of love accompanied as well by torment—the torment of comprehending the incomprehensible.

Freedom cannot be shared as a mutually chosen object, nor can two persons exercise their freedom in the same manner.

The state of mind of freedom in each person is different. In most of us it is a fleeting state of mind. Freedom is uncertainty. The exercise of freedom is a journey into the unknown. It can never be secured.

In creation, there are no sides. One does not choose this

over that in the act of creation. There is no opposition in creation. In spite of the fact that what has been created has often been destroyed, burned or condemned, the act of creation itself is not based on vengeance or opposition. Creation is altruistic. It is we in our ultimate state of freedom reaching for new horizons. It is a confirmation of the individual's infinite potential to ask, to seek, to bring together/exclude infinite thoughts, things, and experiences in infinitely different combinations. Freedom is a confirmation of freedom, not a blueprint for utopia. It is through more people reaching to such heights that universal and moral principles can be upheld.

The destroyers of that which has been created have usually been those who have not had, who have not been given the opportunity to either truly taste the creations of others or to create themselves. The forces of destruction cannot be destroyed for that would require even more forces of destruction.

The forces of destruction in each and every one of us are reinforced by opposing choices and can only wither away in the face of creativity and its ensuing beauty.

November 25, 1986, Marburg

IN DEFENSE OF TRAITORS

X

C.J. Patterson, 1917

I WANT YOU
FOR U.S. ARMY
NEAREST RECRUITING STATION

Treachery can be pleasing, but traitors are despicable.
Miguel de Cervantes

I.

The lowest of the low in any society is a traitor. Changing, deserting or even criticizing one's side meets with hatred. While the enemy may often arouse respect, the traitor is always condemned. Traitors are considered so despicable that even the lowest place in Dante's *Inferno* is set aside for the betrayers of their relatives and country. Carnal sinners, murderers, blasphemers, perverts, seducers, sorcerers, thieves and hypocrites have more privileged positions in Dante's hell than traitors.

II.

We expect a person to stick to his side. A traitor is forced to leave his community. He leaves a structure marked by strong feelings of belonging. It is through such feelings that life in a community becomes meaningful. Should one choose no longer to belong, it is a blow to the others. Rather than reappraising themselves, the community bonds even more firmly and condemns the traitor. Communities are rarely inclined to question their own acts, sacrifices and ties. For in such questioning, their resolve is tested and threatened. After years of marching and singing together, after years of patting each other on the back, after having suffered together, celebrated together, a question or even a hint of what might be taken as doubt is a threat to us all, a threat to our present, past and future. That threat is personified in the traitor.

III.

Though the historical development of the community may be full of contradictions and inconsistencies, the traitor is always judged on the basis of the present moment. One is always a traitor to the present. The present structure and the balance of power determines who the traitor will be. The "traitor" may have been very consistent with the past history of the community. If the community has collectively changed, however, it is that individual who will be the odd man out. Looking at the history of the Soviet Union, for example, we see one leader after another condemning each other as traitors. No matter who was condemning who, the party and the citizens have always joined the chorus. All together, in one voice, Long live the Revolution! Long live the Party!

What we are actually saying, what we have always said is LONG LIVE THE PRESENT MOMENT AND OUR PLACE IN IT.

So be it for those who refuse to go along.

IV.

In another sense, the real traitor is us. It is the masses. It is those who always follow the official, the given line. The president of the football club declares one day that the colours of the team should actually not be red and blue but crimson and purple. "In the past," he says, "when the club was first founded a hundred and fifty years ago, the dyes that were used in the uniforms actually resembled purple and crimson. Our true colours are purple and crimson not red and blue." And what happens? Everybody votes unanimously to change colours. We are always changing colours.

Human history is one instance after another of us changing sides. All major revolutions are minority revolutions. They have been carried out, made possible, by the action of the minority. The majority supported these very radical historical changes only after the fact. Once we revered Kings, Sultans and Czars and despised anti-monarchists. Then, in the name of the republic they became our traitors.

Tomorrow?

We are always changing ideologies, methods of raising children, moral attitudes, tastes, habits, organizations, life styles, institutions, borders, spouses, loved ones, favourite songs and food.

In acting collectively, we are always right. It is the individual that we attack. Those who do not go along are condemned. We single them out in history books, we single them out in our neighbourhood. We single them out in sermons and presidential addresses. We make the names of the traitors live. They live together in the collective consciousness of a community and along with heroes strengthen the bonds among its members. We suppress and hide our doubts when we imagine the traitor as an individual and the misery he has been condemned to by us. The more we condemn the traitor the more dogmatic we become. We question less and less, become more and more totalitarian, and eventually understand nothing.

In our confirmation of a side, we feel strength and pride.

We can withstand torture, we can die for our cause knowing our name will be revered. We know that the marching band of history will cheer us on, that we will go down in history. Rarely does that happen to the traitor who feels a responsibility to speak his mind and go his own way. Branded as being on the payroll of the enemy, he is alone. He has always been alone, and knows that he will always be alone. In our totalitarianism we destroy the individual. We rarely tolerate individual freedom because we fear it. We fear that freedom will destroy the very structures that give order and meaning to our lives. We make traitors because we are obedient and follow blindly. Because we are so weak, we are totalitarian. A belief in the self, a belief in the human would lead to a society with no traitors, for we would have no reason to be afraid ourselves.

"If you don't like it, you can leave," we say, "leave for the land of the enemy." The traitor suffers individually while the masses hold on to their illusions often at the expense of critical thought. Who then is the traitor?

December 2, 1986; March 17, 1987, Marburg

THREE EXAMPLES OF HOW
"GREAT CONTEMPORARY CIVILIZATIONS"
RELATE TO THEIR FAMOUS TRAITORS

Case 1: The United States of America (In God We Trust)

vs.

Ezra Pound (Poet and traitor)

Put in solitary confinement in Italy after World War II by U.S. forces for having appealed through radio broadcasts to the American soldiers not to raise arms against Italy.

Brought to Washington, tried for treason, found guilty.

Instead of prison, sent to St. Elizabeth's mental hospital for 12 years.

Diagnosis: Treason committed due to insanity.

Released by the U.S. government after pressure from leading American poets.

He returned immediately to Italy.

Case 2: The Union of Soviet Socialist Republics (Workers of the World, Unite)

vs.

Leon Trotsky Bordonovitch (Hero and traitor)

Banished from his country, declared a non-person.

Having followed him all over the world from Istanbul to Copenhagen and eventually Mexico, a hired killer of Stalin's worker's state was eventually successful in lodging a fatal ice pick in Trotsky's head.

WHAT HAPPENED TO THE MURDERER?

In prison for about ten years he went to Moscow after his release, was given a hero's welcome by the Communist Party and,

DECORATED with the highest MEDAL in the land by BREZHNEV.

Trotsky was rehabilitated by Chairman Gorbachov who condemned Stalin and Brezhnev for their errors.

Case 3: United Kingdom (God Save the Queen)
U.S.S.R. (Workers of the World Unite)
U.S.A. (In God We Trust)
France (Liberte, Equalite, Fraternite)
vs.
The Third Reich (Deutschland Über Alles)
and,
Walter Rudolph Hess (Nazi, traitor)
Helped write *Mein Kampf*,
Second in succession to Adolph Hitler.

Took part with Hitler in the abortive Beer Hall Putsch, escaped to Austria, returned of his own free will back to Germany to serve out jail sentence.

Surprised the world by flying secretly to Scotland at the height of World War II to make a peace proposal to the English.

Condemned by Hitler as a traitor. Locked up by Churchill as a prison-of-war. Sanity questioned at the Nuremberg Trials. Confined to life in prison.

Spent 41 years at Spandau Prison, 41 years in SOLITARY CONFINEMENT. Last 21 years as the sole prisoner.

(He was the world's most carefully guarded inmate with English, French, American and Soviet security guards all keeping watch).

The world still does not know his story which has been carefully guarded. Said to have committed suicide in 1987. Prison torn down immediately thereafter.

Hear no Evil.
Speak no Evil.
See no Evil.

January 2, 1986, Marburg

DEATH FORGETTING

XI

The Cyclists, Jose Guadalupe Pasada, 1889

You will die not because you're ill but because you're alive.
Lucius Seneca

I.

We think the least about that which is most imminent. It can happen any second to anyone and to all. It is bound to happen. Death will happen and each second brings us closer to it. Our biggest denial of life is our denial of death. We put ourselves into a mental straight jacket rarely thinking that we are mortal, that we will die. We rarely have the feeling that each moment that we live, experience, smell, see, touch will not happen again. What makes life very special, very unique is that everything happens only once. That realization can only come through the consciousness of death. One who is not conscious of death is also not conscious of living.

Yet, we are engaged in a constant process of "death forgetting."

II.

Awareness of the death process is a realization of the fleeting beauty of life. It is also an awareness of the permanence of beauty. For it is not time or beauty, but the individual that is fleeting. Any thought or activity that excludes death leads to attempts to possess life. Many relationships are based on this impossibility, the lie, that life can be possessed. This phenomenon is best exemplified by the existence and use of the word "forever." Stopping death by cancelling time is not only a sign of greed for our own individual lives but also an attempt to possess all there is. There is no instinct or necessity which dictates that we must speak, make love, take photographs, succeed, create works of art, be altruistic, be sadistic, love others or hate others. Whether and how we do such things is up to us. One can exist and still be aware of the beauty and wonders of life without doing any of the above, or one can do all of the above and still not be aware. With respect to the so-called "purpose of life," all our missions have been self-imposed. All explanations of life have been an attempt to find a design, a purpose as defined by us.

The purpose of life is life until death. It is ludicrous for anyone to attempt universal theories. They will be disproved again and again.

III.

In the compartmentalization, specialization and apartheid of life since the Industrial Revolution, anything to do with death has been pushed to the fringes and marginalized. Not only do we no longer share the deaths of people close to us —our neighbours, the grocer, the teacher— we also do not even see funeral processions, burials, hangings, cremations. After not seeing a semi-anonymous person that one is accustomed for years to seeing almost every day (bus driver on route to work, person who takes money at your usual gas station, elevator operator at the office building, stamp seller at the post office...) we forget about the person. "The Show Must Go On" includes not only the theatre but us as well. We have all become part of the show. What is not on stage might as well be dead. It does not exist. We are pre-occupied with life as we see it on stage. Our stage. The stage according to us.

One of our most fundamental mental processes is death forgetting. Especially present day western society (and through it the rest of the world) is being shaped in such a way as to even forget about aging. The sociological position of the two extremes —young and old— has radically changed in the past hundred years. Formerly, babies and children were in such a position that they should be seen and not heard. They were not recognized as individuals in their own right. Only when they became adults did they become individuals. Even children's clothing with a distinctive style is a recent development. One need only look at nineteenth century paintings to realize that. On the other hand, the elderly formerly had a very prominent place in society. They were the learned, the powerful, the wise. They were proud of their age. Now, we have the opposite situation. It is the old people who should not be seen as well as not heard. Children, on the other hand, have now become sacred individuals. Special laws are passed to protect children, to promote children's rights. None exist for the old.

A whole range of technology, literature, psychological research and legislative action has spotlighted the role of children so that they have in many ways become the most important persons of our species. While the elderly are being shut up in various quarters, babies are now taken along to just about anywhere. The sense and spirit of participation and communication that society shows to children does not exist for the elderly, who are regarded more and more as a burden that one must put up with. And to go back to the clothing example, while children now have their own particular clothes and fashion, the elderly no longer do. They have lost their unique clothing of the past century and are now encouraged to look young, dress young. Aging, old age, and death are marginalized, eliminated.

IV.

In the process of death forgetting we lose our freedom of action. Living as if we always will, we become lazy and fail to actively participate in life with life. We fail to act, to move, to discover, to ask and to find. We fail to be courageous. In forgetting about death, we become part of a monotonous standardized existence of our own making. Once this standardized monotony becomes a way of life, we not only try to protect it, but also discourage individuals from trying to change it. The apple cart must not be upset. The compliance with a seemingly never-changing existence gives us a sense of security. This very much resembles the security of the so-called obsessive compulsive neurotic person for whom everything must be just so in order for him not to feel any anxiety. In the same way, we as a species, avoid fear through death forgetting.

Death for man has been the greatest unknown. It has also been the source of the greatest fear. Our way of reducing fear of the unknown has been through religion —by discussing and making explicit the afterlife. Hell and punishment can be avoided by deeds which will send one to heaven, paradise, elysium.

The secularization of society and the accompanying atheism has also reinforced death forgetting. By making the unknown knowable, we reduce fear. For many, the perfect life is that society in which everything can be predicted. The explicit quest of science has been exactly that—to predict and control. In this sense, science and medicine also promote the process of death forgetting through the paraphernalia of healthy living.

Death forgetting leads us to a comfortable, secure state. We need only preoccupy ourselves with daily pleasures and problems. As one problem is always replaced by another, no problem is that deep as to have an existential effect on the individual. Death forgetting leads to a state of not having any existential anxiety.

V.

By tasting the apple Adam lost his blissful, secure place in paradise. He also became a mortal with fear of death. It is the existence of death, the realization that death may come at any moment, however, that ultimately makes men free. No one can rule over, predict or control death. We have birth control. There is no death control.

Freedom is praised by everyone. Few however, speak about how difficult it is to be free or how few of us, and especially those who think of themselves as being free, are free. Freedom in its ultimate sense is the ability to live with fear, the courage to face fear, confront fear. Those who guarantee for us a fear-free society and life also take away our freedom. Those, to whom we trade in our freedom to be free from fear, become the new sources of fear.

Just as security and servitude go hand in hand, so too do freedom and fear. Fear is part of the human condition. It cannot be eradicated though we allow ourselves to be lulled, lullabyed and deluded. A person who does not fear is like a person who cannot blush. A person who cannot blush has no sense of ethics. A person who does not fear has no fundamental sense of life and death. Death forgetting is a futile attempt to forget fear. It amounts to a total denial of the reality that man is mortal.

VI.

The opposite of life is not death. The opposite of death is birth. Birth and death are a part of the process we refer to as life. Death is as much a part of life as birth. "That's life," we say upon a death. "Here's to life," we say upon a birth. Denying either birth or death is tantamount to denying life. By denying death, by rebelling against death, by seeking immortality, we are denying life. Thus, to say, as Freud did for example, that one has two instincts — one for life and the other for death — is nonsense. In explaining life we do not need this Manichaenism. There is no need to resort to a duality in trying to explain the existence of the forces of life and death, of good and evil. Death and birth are contained in life. It is only our perception, our fear, that has made such a duality.

There is no so-called battle of life and death. Life is birth and death. If there were such a battle we certainly have lost all encounters. Yet, poets, doctors, politicians and priests keep on talking about it. We are all afraid of death and think of it as a battle that we may eventually win. Many of us in our own fashion are like the Spanish explorer Ponce de Leon seeking the fountain of youth in Florida.

Our most totalitarian act as a species is death forgetting. By acting as if we will live forever, by acting as if the earth will exist forever, by having no explicit consciousness of the process of birth and death in us, in each and every one of us, by thinking that the show will go on forever, we fail to be free. For any attempt at freedom, any state of freedom is immediately accompanied by a sense of death. Freedom means to do, to imagine anything and everything that we want. To ask what has not been asked, to dare what has not been dared. It is a quest of the unknown. The quest of the unknown is dangerous. Danger in its ultimate meaning is death.

The quest also means living with fear, being afraid but still going on. One loses one's freedom when one gives in to fear and is afraid to act, afraid to follow one's vision. It is normal to fear. But it is not necessary to give in to fear, to give up thinking and asking. Being reminded of death or danger is being reminded of our freedom. It is knowing that we are exercising that freedom, that we are engaged in the act of being free. Any other feeling is a sense of false security. It is a totalitarian control over reality in which we deny ourselves the exercise of life by denying death.

As the bell tolls louder and louder for our planet and species we look the other way, are more and more pursuing healthier lifestyles, buckling up for safety, avoiding passive smoking, seeking the lowest cholesterol diet.

In postponing our death we become blinder to life.

Winter, 1984 Vienna; Fall, 1989, Kea

BEWARE OF THE ARTIST!

XII

Pre-historic cave painting, Serra, Libya

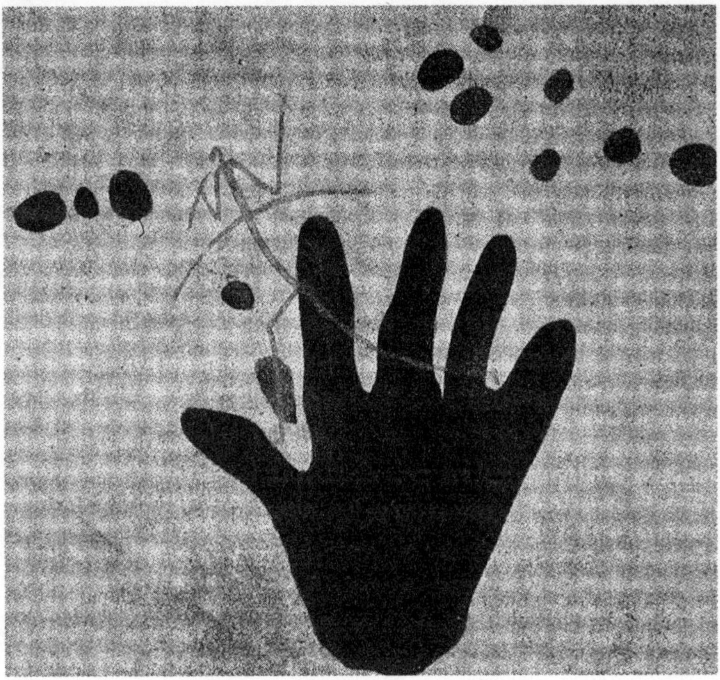

One cannot serve both God and Mammon.
St. Matthew

I.

Why does one write? Paint? Compose music?

The creator lives intensely. The weight of the universe, the depth of infinity are enclosed in his thoughts and emotions. He not only has something new to say but is also looking for a new way of saying it. He is looking for a new language. He has fantasy. Language and fantasy combine in infinite forms expressing life within as well as life beyond. He is a sufferer. In order to live he must create.

Through creation he reduces his suffering.

The creative work is a straight-jacket on the act of living. Creative activity prevents one from going mad, committing suicide. Rilke's advice to an aspiring poet was that he might be one, only if he could not keep himself from writing. There is the urge, the need to create. It is a lonely, individual effort. The creator does not share his life. He shuts himself. Eventually he displays the created object. Each creator escapes to his nook in order to fantasize, to go into depth. He goes away from others into his private individual space.

The creator shows his intensity for life through his work —be it music, painting, writing.

In many cases there are those who are dedicated to him. For him to create his work, they sacrifice, they serve. They cater to his whims and desires. They exist for him, whereas he exists for his work. Creation is a desperate act undertaken by those who live intensely and who rarely share in love with others. We do not create in our everyday lives. We do not create through our everyday relationships. The artist only creates in avoidance after having run away. We have not been able to create in communion with each other.

II.

The printed novel, recorded music, reproduced art are, on the whole, examples of dictated standards. Rather than being created and shared, art is produced and consumed. The artist, in his inclination to reach and excel above everybody, reinforces both for him and for each one of us, a totalitarian order.

What difference is there between a "creator" who allows himself to compete with others, who allows his works to be mass produced, who allows himself to be advertised and the Soviet worker hero, the brick layer Stakhanov, who worked more, better and faster than all others? A "creator" who allows himself to join the international hit parade of prizes, competitions and advertisements is just as much a symbol of totalitarianism as Stalin's Stakhanov. "Best-sellers" in art are another form of the standard McDonald's hamburger, tasting the same in Arkansas, as in Brussels, Hong-Kong and Istanbul. Given the infinite potential and possibility for creation, there is absolutely no reason for one work to be compared with and subsequently proclaimed to be superior to others. It sets mass standards and tastes, killing the possibility of recognizing and encouraging a potentially infinite amount of other created works, each with something new to say and saying it in a new way.

It is an aspect of our totalitarian tendency to not only choose and order what is best in art for our particular century, but even go back across centuries in our search for the best, biggest and brightest. The act of creation is no longer privately exhilarating or fulfilling. We are long past the age when the creator remained anonymous. Most important now is recognition. For some, even immediate recognition is not enough. It must be for all time. We have a tendency of wanting to dominate history, of seeking to be the greatest that there ever was. In creation there can never be such a thing as the greatest.

The American psychiatrist Robert Lifton holds that the motivating force behind all our actions is to seek immortality. He cites four types: religious (the eternal soul), genetic (our seed living on through our offspring), creative (our names will live on through our works), and historical (with each action, each one of us is creating and becoming part of history). Again, another typical contemporary view that man must somehow belong forever, leave his imprint in history and dominate the future. Nothing about love, joy, sharing or merely playing. The world in the future is important only in so far as we can be remembered.

In creating, there can be no comparison or ranking, only the possibility for profound experience.

The artist of our century, in his desire to reach and excel above all, and for all time, reinforces, both for him and each one of us, a tendency toward totalitarianism.

III.

He who only expresses through his art is a meek person. He chooses to hide behind his created object. He removes himself from those living their everyday lives. Through his created objects, he comments, criticizes and suffers in the name of others. He becomes alienated and bitter. Creation becomes condemning rather than liberating. Creation not shared becomes creation possessed. The creator, by limiting his creation to his created object, makes and treats us as his objects. By appraising, accepting and applauding the creator's objects, we reinforce the condemnation of our everyday lives. Because we cannot, because we do not create through our everyday lives, creators are segregated, selfish, sacrificing and look down at us in contempt and/or bitterness.

Between the creator and the audience stands a "middleman" responsible for bringing the people and the product together. He judges on the basis of profit, ideology and taste. There are many types of middlemen. There was the art commissar of the party in the socialist countries who decided what was to be exhibited before the public. There is the arts council of a city that chooses what is to be shown. There are the advisors to the multi-million dollar tax evading foundations who chose to support certain works over others. And there are the managers in multimedia companies who manufacture, package and distribute art and artists as if they were toothpaste or canned soup.

In all such cases, the distinction made between the artist and the people leads to a one-sided relationship in which one is performing and consumed by others. This removes art from the spontaneity of life where we do things together. For art, in essence, is not a performance or an object but a mutual sharing of an experience, a partaking of a process. This does not negate for example, the distinction between a violin soloist and the audience. It does not mean that the audience must also be violin players and know the musical score. It refers to the realization that what is played is very much a part of all our lives and not something that belongs to the "realm of music." Everything is in the realm of life. The music is just as much a part of our lives as it is the player's and the composer's. It is not something that we merely appreciate, approve, compare or consume. It is not something with which we become more cultured.

The moment we make a distinction between the artist's world and ours is also the moment when we create the stage for the totalitarianism of art in terms of not only the performance and performer, but also the role of art in our lives.

Art can neither be expanding nor oppressive. The perception of art as being something out there, rather than within each and every one of us, gives art its oppressive nature. It is only when we are one with art that it can be fulfilling and expanding, making us deeply aware of experiences in the multi-faceted reality of the universe.

Art in recent centuries has become more and more a specialty executed by specialists. It is removed from the people, removed from life. The artists have become professionals who execute, rather than persons who create, just as those in sports perform instead of play.

In becoming good at one thing we have also lost the total feeling of life. In becoming good at one thing we have mercilessly driven ourselves in execution and often with the belief that the means justifies the end. The means however often directly negates life, the harmony of life and art, the harmony of art and man. In abstracting art from life and transforming it into a specialized performance for an audience, we try to achieve a controlled situation in which art becomes predictable and totalitarian.

Not only has art become a speciality, it has also become an industry. Many people make their living from working in the arts industry as technicians, advisors, bureaucrats, public relation experts, agents and tax consultants.

The industrial civilization has produced a society in which people have one particular predominant activity, their work. Outside of the execution of this activity we spend our time watching others perform. We live in societies in which we are always performing for each other but never together. In contrast, it is always of interest for anthropologists to see people from non-Western cultures spontaneously expressing themselves in the various forms of art as a community.

IV.

With the transition from community *(Gemeinde)* to society (*Gesellschaft*) we have, as individuals, given up activities with respect to the various expressions of life. Musical instruments for example left our houses to be replaced by records and discs. The family no longer makes music together. We still dance, but it is no longer an expression of our lives. Our dances come and go out of fashion in accordance with the dictates of the music industry. The theatre, once an integral part of the community's way of life, is now either sheer entertainment or a cathartic substitution for lives that we do not, cannot, are not free to lead. Same with poetry. Once very much a part of our daily life and conversation, it has now become so marginal that very few either write, recite or listen to poetry.

Outside our work, we have taken up what are called pasttimes or hobbies with which we engage ourselves in our "free time." Thus, there are those whose hobby is to play the violin or paint. However, there is a critical difference between the person who takes it up as a hobby and the person of yesteryear who also played the violin. Then, it was very much a part of everyday life involving the family and community with a sense of tradition. Today, the person playing the violin is an individual looking for substance and meaning in his alienated life. He is doing his own thing in his free time. This situation has arisen from the abstraction of the person from life around him or even from life itself.

Mere technical perfection and specialization in art is tantamount to perfection in making love. It is tantamount to totalitarianism, a subjugation of the forces of life. It is a denial of art, a denial of the spiritual community of man and a denial of the art of living.

V.

In removing the artist from our midst we have allowed for art to become dictated to us. We have turned art over to governments and companies. Without us, art has become mechanical, alienated, lifeless. Or, the other side of the coin, it has become (but only for a minute minority of isolated individuals) an intense revolt at the state of our being. In both cases, it is a comment about us by artists either exalted or in exile. Art is without us, as we are without art.

"There will no longer be any poets when we all become poets, when, in our everyday lives we all live as poems," says my friend Resit Ergener.

January 21, 1987, Marburg

DISAGREEMENT FOREVER

XIII

The meeting of two men each of whom thinks
that the other is more important
Paul Klee, "The Men Meeting," 1903

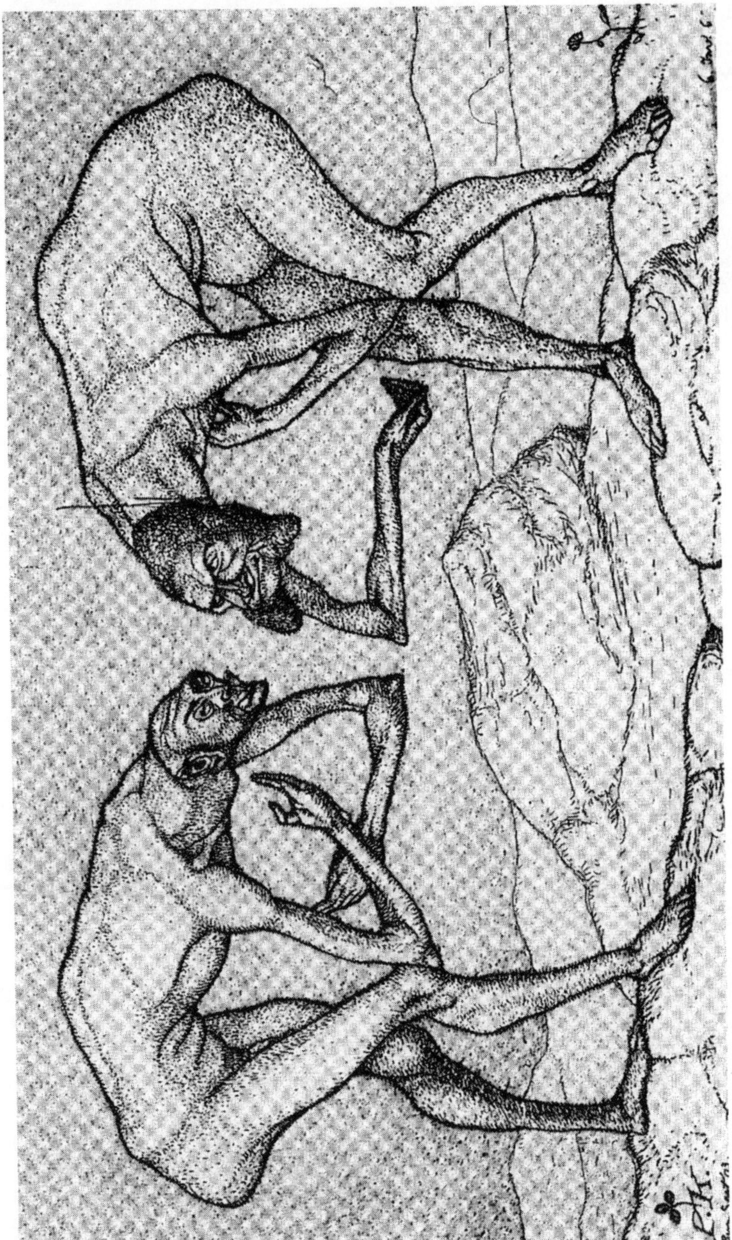

If everyone pulled in the same direction the earth would keel over.
Yiddish proverb

I.

We need confirmation of thought, opinion, taste, experience. It makes us feel secure both as individuals and with each other. The need for agreement dominates the truth. We agree for the sake of security and sacrifice the truth. In agreeing we collectively share and confirm. What is not agreed upon remains isolated and forgotten, rarely becoming a part of our common culture and civilization. In the course of our everyday lives we find it convenient to agree. It makes little sense to disagree if an argument can hinder the day's progress. Agreement is totalitarian.

II.

We frequently say, "yes" and mean "no," just to get on with the day. We establish bonds by agreeing. We like those we agree with and dislike those we don't. In general, we spend more time agreeing than disagreeing. Happy marriages, long lasting friendships, positive working atmospheres, relationships between rulers and the ruled can only be lasting when there is agreement. If something goes wrong, the task of the counselor, teacher, industrial psychologist, public relations expert is to get the parties to agree again. There is usually little inclination toward fundamental changes. In spite of the misery, injustice and unhappiness in the world, in spite of living in a world in which we are destroying ourselves and other species, we still agree with the establishment, with the books, with each other. In harmony we go on together. The false sense of harmony in agreement, reinforces the status quo. It is a collision course to catastrophe. Still, we just don't want to be disagreeable. We tend to agree with each other and authority until almost the very end, when everybody tears at each other's throats. Agreement ends not with a disagreement but with total chaos. Until then, we dare not utter negative statements. We are our own censors in our own self-built prisons.

III.

Agreement is a process in which we imitate and internalize order that is already given in the hierarchical totalitarian society. The socialization process that we all go through on our way to adulthood is a process in which we are taught to agree. We learn to agree with all the rules ranging from those in simple children's games to the laws of the establishment. There is no room in the socialization process, not a single instance, which allows for disagreement. It is considered friendly to agree. In the family, at school, in religion or government, it is bad, impolite, dangerous to disagree.

Even in disagreement we agree to disagree. The ordained thinkers, academicians and sages of the establishment agree to disagree, giving them a sense of false security to go on with their work without worry of severe criticism or ostracism. It also leads to complacency, both about their work and the work of others, with little or no fundamentally critical questions being asked. Can truth be shared? Agreed upon? No.

IV.

Ultimately, what we all share in common are questions. Our paths may cross in the process of seeking answers. We may recognize that "look" in each other that comes from questioning and searching. However, the moment we establish a bond in that look, the moment the bond becomes greater than the searching experience, the moment the bond impedes the free flow of the search, then we lose all freedom for the quest of the unattainable. We are no longer free. In belonging we agree. We become one in agreement. Then, not only do we all start asking the same questions, but also seek the same answers. In holy books and textbooks, in constitutions and universal declarations the answers are recorded, codified and become sacrosanct, unquestionable (i.e. "We hold these truths to be self evident.") Additional questions are considered to come from the heretic, the public enemy, the ignorant, the non-realistic or the mad man.

V.

In most cases, an agreement is a lie, a sign of mistrust. In conversation, often without really listening to the other, we say that we agree, we say "Yes, yes," and nod just so we can get to speak ourselves and say what we mean. In such daily conversation agreement is just a guise for the person to stop the other from speaking and declaring his opinion. Negotiations between warring countries, employers and labour unions, landlords and tenants are all settled through agreements. In such cases an agreement actually means an acceptance of the views and conditions of the strong by the weak.

Those who do not vie for power, who are not struggling against each other, rarely need to agree. Rather, like leaves falling from a tree, they float together in harmoniously improvised relationships. A young couple agreeing on a marriage promise each other things that negate the spirit of attachment. The marriage vow is more a renunciation of freedom than a confirmation of love. It is an agreement of mutual duties opposed to any sense of altruism that accompanies love. How can one agree to become friends or lovers? Such things happen spontaneously. We become friends and lovers. The love bond is an unwritten contract with two carbon copies. Yet, with both copies saying different things in different languages, though with affinity.

VI.

Why cannot there be disagreement, accompanied by trust, security and belief in the other at the same time? Why are divergence and disagreement taken as signs of rejection? Why does it seem to be a catastrophe when two persons who have agreed on almost everything for years disagree strongly on a particular subject, with this taken as signs of not having known each other at all? Or how is it possible that two different persons could really have agreed with each other for so long on matters ranging from taste to ideology? Why does being with each other mean agreeing with each other? Why is a harmonious relationship looked upon as one of agreement? The positive proton and the negative electron of the atom—do they not also have a harmonious relationship? And to think that there is also anti-matter in harmony with matter.

Freedom is a function of disagreement. It is a process of never having to agree. The confirmation of freedom is in not seeking to agree.

Agreement stops a process. It freezes things. It is a brake on creativity. Critical thought means encouraging disagreement. We are totalitarian and disrespectful to ourselves when we encourage agreement rather than disagreement. If nature is at harmony in and through conflict, so we too can disagree. We owe it to ourselves. In disagreeing we will stop lying.

February 16, 1987, Marburg

GOALS AGAINST LIFE

XIV

Pre-historic cave painting, Zimbabwe.
At the bottom, someone has been sacrificed. Others, trying to reach the goddess by climbing up the ladder that turns into a snake are about to fall back down to earth.

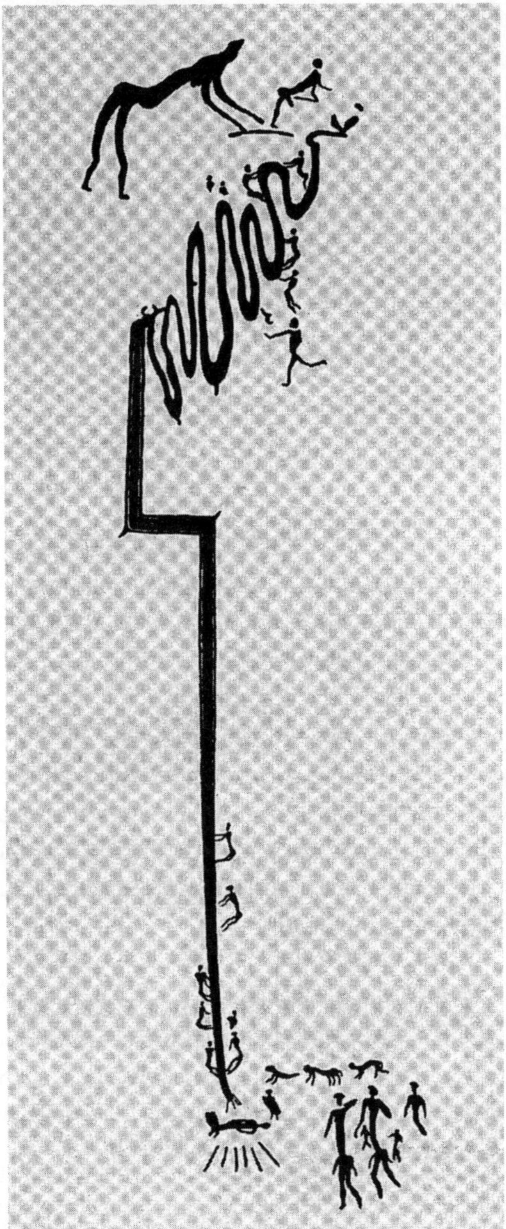

They asked the moon:
What would you like the most?
The moon answered:
That the sun would disappear and always stay
behind the clouds.
Feriddedin-i Attar

I.

"Plan your life. Pursue your goals. Know what you want out of life. Don't let anything get in your way. With determination and discipline there isn't anything you can't accomplish. You certainly have the talent for it."

So it goes. Parents, priests, psychologists, best friends and you to yourself, repeating, believing in all the above. The absurdity of all this struck home one day when I read the following: "She has fixed goals," went the ad for a bank written under the picture of a good looking middle-aged woman with a determined look in her face, " and we will help her get there."

Banks, governments, businesses, professional associations, those who run and plan the structure of society, all want us to have goals. They want us to be determined in their pursuit and thereby predictable. Through our goals they exercise a totalitarian control over us.

II.

"Understanding, predicting and controlling behaviour" is the unwritten logo of our social sciences – especially psychology as a behavioural science. That is the purpose of psychology. Whose interests does it serve? The collected information with respect to our behaviour is the basis of power for the post-industrial (post-modern) establishment(s). Information about our behaviour enables them to control society, to control their "citizens," to control and exploit us. Information is power. Therefore, for instance, in some Scandinavian countries and Germany there is resistance against a national census.

The collection of information is one of the main activities of companies who meticulously classify and share with each other almost everything there is to know about us. Every time we fill out an application blank, apply for a credit card, join a book club, we provide information.

Isn't there anything about which we have no opinions? The establishment guides us to have an opinion about everything that they plan for us. Isn't it curious that there has never been an opinion poll the results of which showed the majority had no opinion? We are coaxed, guided, pressured to choose this over that.

Rulers don't like surprises. The element of surprise in our century is fast disappearing. Surprises shock rulers. Surprises upset both our plans and theirs. Surprises stand in the way of goals.

The establishment knows how much we'll spend for what the coming year, who will take his vacation where and for how long, and even the demand for lawyers services that could be needed for those who might seek divorce during their vacations. Market researchers, psychologists, sociologists try to understand and predict human behaviour and goals on the basis of information they collect about us. Subsequently, they try to control and influence behaviour through various methods of social engineering and public opinion management. Having established a certain pattern, foreseen a typical type of behaviour, they seek to reinforce that behaviour so that they can profit from it. The manufacture of almost everything from chocolate bars to frying pans, from prophylactics to bathing suits is based on our predictability superimposed by the establishment. We are even predictable in those types of behaviours that once used to be considered the most imaginative. Our crimes for instance have become so common-place, so devoid of the unexpected, so vulgarly predictable in terms of plan, object and method that police know years in advance the types of crimes to expect and what equipment they need for its prevention.

Our freedom is in our unpredictability. A big question mark over freedom in western countries arises precisely from the government's expectation of mass predictability from its citizens. In Sweden, for example, on the basis of mass behavioural analyses and statistical forecasts, the establishment is forever engaged in social engineering and future planning. Nothing is left to chance (Even some toilets are provided with a specific space and pen for writing graffiti).

In spite of the fact that we may think that we set up and follow our own individual goals, they are actually, in most cases, already determined by the existing order and our place in it. Our "clothes" are usually cut and ready to wear.

Intelligence agencies like the CIA have long prepared psychological profiles about foreign agents, enemies and potential terrorists—their movements and motivations, likes, dislikes, weaknesses. Now, we are all listed. Police collect information in the name of crime prevention. Political parties monitor our beliefs and behaviour through public opinion polls. Companies analyze our consumption patterns and taste. They all want to know and manipulate our behaviour, our plans, our goals. We are under complete scrutiny.

III.

Goals are against freedom and creativity. Yet, society is more and more organized with a hierarchy of people whose special job is to help us plan our goals, to support us in reaching our goals.

Choosing the "proper goal" for one's life has become so important in this century that we even have "scientific" methods of determining the career for which one is best suited. Psychologists have developed various instruments which are said to show whether a youngster has an inclination to be, for instance, a preacher or a musician. These personality inventories are especially widely used in secondary schools in the U.S. and also in those countries which follow the trends set in that country. Just as in the case of a specific part for a machine, so a human is also expected to "fit" one of the professions of the given social order. Once the goal and the person fit each other, the profession and the person also become merged with one another in many ways.

We relate more and more to each other through our goals, labels, professions, rather than as one human to another. The nature of the relationship is often decided not on the basis of the individual personalities (which have been repressed anyway by professional identification) but by mutual interest and the affinity of our "goals" as determined by the values, interests and the balance of power within the existing social order. We make deals rather than meet persons. "What can I get out of this relationship?" comes up in the mind at the very moment one says "Hello." The most frequently exchanged information when people first meet is solicited through the question, "What do you do?" rather than the non-inquisitive way of address of more traditional societies. Relationships are determined on the basis of explicit goals rather than on the universal "communality" of the human. Because we all pursue many goals, we also have many different identifications at the same time. But in each case, the result or the goal is greater than the person. It also governs, determines the nature of relationships between persons.

Ideological convictions are another example of goal pursuing behaviour. After having identified ourselves with an ideology, we begin to "grow" to "shape" ourselves in the image of the ideology, in the image of its proponents, its heroes. Often, we go against our own common sense and experience. Often, we don't perceive what we see and hear. More and more we mold ourselves both in physical appearance and mental paradigm to the image of the ideology. Finally, we come to such a point that ideology becomes even more important than life itself. Religion has also played a similar role in history. And once we have been successfully molded into the model of the establishment, we express ambitions, wishes, desires and above all goals that are completely in keeping with what is expected and desired of us.

Pleasure, belief, love and as the Turkish poet Nazım Hikmet said, "To live in awe like a child." Can they be planned?

IV.

Any fixed goal, no matter what the object, is totalitarian. Nothing is greater than life. One cannot have a goal other than that of living. We are perhaps the only species that has the power of taking one's own life away—not as a species-specific behaviour as in the case of the lemmings for example, but rather as the result of a conscious act. We have the power to choose to live or die. If we indeed must use the word goal, our only goal can be that of living, of living as full a life as possible. To impose anything else on life is totalitarian.

All goal-pursuing behaviour is totalitarian. Psychologists have carried out many deprivation experiments with mice to ascertain the strength of certain basic goal-seeking drives such as hunger, thirst, sex and the parental instinct (for the female mouse only!). What is measured is the time it takes for a mouse to learn a maze, at the end of which is usually food or whatever the animal has been deprived of. The sooner the goal is reached, the stronger the drive is said to be. We too, well established psychological theories say, manifest goal-directed behaviour as a function of our drives. It is also claimed that only after the satiation of such basic primitive drives can one have higher order goals (first level: food, clothing, shelter; next level: love, security; highest level: self-realization). All our behaviour, it is said, is based on need reduction. It is to reduce the above needs that the human is set into motion, motivated to do this and that with respect to reaching particular goals. This widely held 20th century theory does not make sense given some fundamental characteristics of human behaviour, such as altruism and voluntarily altered states of consciousness and suicide. Much of our behaviour runs counter to the goal-oriented need hierarchy theories of psychology.

All goal-pursuing behaviour is totalitarian because we allow the goal to determine the nature of the behaviour, rather than behaviour spontaneously evolving in a dialectical relationship with the environment to lead onto new unexpected behaviours. Whether one pursues specific goals or not, is like the difference between marching with a military band or participating in an improvised jam session.

V.

Spontaneity is unpredictable. The "mystery" of the homo sapiens, a characteristic setting the human apart from other living things, is that its actions are unpredictable. The life course of plants is, to a great degree, predetermined. Animals also are subject to what ethologists call species-specific behaviours or fixed action patterns which are predictable. It is only when we come to the most recently evolved species —the homo sapiens— that we find a dominance of behaviour unsolicited by any specific environmental stimuli. It is only to the human that philosophers attribute a "free will." Yet, we have become prisoners of ourselves. Bits and pieces of the human mosaic are transformed to social codes and expectations which in turn become fixed goals. Their attainment gives direction and often meaning to our lives. In the pursuit of such fixed goals we begin to imitate. Day in and day out we imitate ourselves and others. Instead of imitating less and becoming more, the more we imitate, the less we become.

Goal-directed purposeful activity is very much a characteristic of species-specific behaviour such as in the mating behaviour of the stickleback fish, imprinting in baby ducklings, salmon returning upstream to the place where they were born to lay their eggs. The only possible species-specific behaviour attributed to homo sapiens is complex language. But, considering that language has the property of coming up with an infinite amount of words from a finite number of letters, thus allowing for freedom and constant change, we have indeed a free repertoire of behaviour. We are not biologically constructed to follow fixed goals, to have fixed actions. It is only the mental paradigms, our mental sets, our self-constructed prisons which are the source of our fixed action or specific goal-oriented behaviour.

VI.

Goal-oriented behaviour gives us the false notion, accompanied by a sense of security and control, that we are directing our lives, that we are the captain of our ship. We are living our lives, yes. Directing them, no! Thousands and thousands of people and chances influence whether we will be dead or alive the next minute. Because we tend to think of the present position of our lives as a point that has been *reached*, we also tend to think that there has been progress up to that point. Looking at the situation after the fact makes it seem inevitable for us to be where we are, almost as if we had planned it, or as if it had been pre-determined. There seems to be a pattern because we tend to pick out only those events, circumstances, actions that reinforce the position that we have reached in our lives today. If we wanted, we could also think of millions of reasons why we should not be where we are. Yet our basic effort is one of always confirming, always trying to find a comprehensible pattern, which makes things seem meaningful rather than mysterious, which gives us a sense of control in fixed time and space rather than oneness with the vastness of the universe.

In thinking that our present state is the result of goal-oriented behaviour, we are actually imposing a totalitarian order on our individual past, just as official history is also an effort to impose a totalitarian order on the collective past.

VII.

Goal-oriented activity implies, when undertaken individually, egocentricism with the person being shut off from other processes taking place in life. On the other hand, when goal-oriented activity is a common process, it implies a standardization of wishes and interests, thereby giving the majority the power to enforce the maintenance of standardization, which is taken to be for the common good. For example, in a primary school classroom, whether it is the pupils who choose their individual goals for the day or whether they choose a common goal for the class, leads either to callous selfishness or group repression. The issue is not who decides the goal (as in the classical totalitarian regimes) or the manipulated processes through which goals are decided (as in western democracies). The issue is the goal in and of itself. It is the goal that binds, that suffocates, that imprisons the individual.

Once one has a fixed goal —a goal to be reached at all costs with dedication, determination and sacrifice— it seems that one has become subordinate to one's goal, that life itself has become subordinate to the goal. Thus we turn our backs to the possibility that we might also do other things—completely other things. We always carry within us the seed for change, the potential to do something completely different. We must welcome changing boats in mid-stream, not fear it as the establishment warns. We must always be open to that possibility, be aware that it exists.

We can, life-long, pursue a dominant form of activity, but not as a fixed goal. In life as well as in love, there are no fixed goals. No contracts. Our activities are a manifestation of an unfathomable pattern, intertwined with the beauty and the mystery of life.

It is surprising how many people indeed reach their goals at the cost of love, going through life like a train on fixed rails and a fixed schedule, or a racing car only making pit stops.

The multi-goal fitted person of our era has drive but lacks intensity. We have goals to buy this, achieve that and to experience yet something else. Through goals we consume life rather than living it. We are no longer one with life. Those who minimize their lives to fixed goals, try to get a hold on the surface of life without becoming one with it.

The opposite is not giving oneself up to the winds of fortune or of letting oneself be claimed by kismet (fate). No!

It is only by letting ourselves flow through life with our thought/emotions that we "find" ourselves.

VIII.

Before embarking on a voyage, first speak with the ancient sailors, listen to and understand the winds, then patiently make a boat and sail. Yet, even then, be open to other dreams, changes, circumstances. Throughout our lives, we limit ourselves to fixed goals, only to get on the local ferry and just travel the distance between two known points. Yet, we create an illusion of freedom and choice, accompanied by a sense of independence. Thus, we carefully study weather reports, ride on the port side on odd numbered days, starboard on holidays, have tea at fixed times, never speak with those who wear glasses, always smile at those who wear green and of course allow ourselves just the slight possibility of a dream about jumping ship and going off to our island one day.

C'est la vie? Our predictably totalitarian lives are an insult to the human spirit.

March 7, 1987, Marburg

ZAP! YOU'RE DEAD
XV

Haus-Rucker-Co., 14 meter inflatable index finger by the motorway to Nuremberg Airport, Symposion Urbanum Nürnberg, 1971. The last remaining bit of the humans on earth after they've destroyed the planet and started living underground.

As automation continues all our organs will wither away-
with the exception of the button pushing finger.
Frank Lloyd Wright

I.

"Let there be light," said God, "and there was light."

On a train from Frankfurt to Paris in 1986, I met two Americans visiting Europe. One of them had a relative, whom she confided in the intimacy of travelling together, was the person responsible for pushing the button in Europe to release, I don't know how many missiles in the case of war against the Soviet Union. The second half of the twentieth century has been referred to as a pill-popping society. We regulate our emotions with pills which is yet another example of totalitarianism. We have also become a "button pushing," "button pressing" society.

We control the world around us with buttons. Button pressing is magic. It is a source of immense power. We make things happen. With each press of the button we reinforce the state of mind that we can make things happen. It is the make-believe world of children ("Zap, you're dead," then playing dead) made real. We can make images, sounds and people appear and disappear. Considering that our knowledge of the world reaches us more and more through images rather than first-hand experience, the image is fast becoming the reality. Children play make believe. They play-act. They know that it's a game. For us, however, it is very much an integral, functional part of our lives—pushing, pressing buttons and making things happen.

We are in totalitarian control.

II.

The button is all-holy, all powerful. We're watching television. The despised military dictator appears on the screen. You swear at him. You sneer at him, take down your pants and show him your ass. We have power over him. We control him (modern voodoo?). It is we that have brought him into the room by pressing a button and we can just as easily make him disappear by pressing the button again. If we especially protest against him while there are others around also watching with us, than our sense of power and control is even more. Our heroic deed against the dictator has been witnessed. It becomes heroic in its having been witnessed. Of course, as you protest, you see in the faces of some others watching with you, a sense of fear. They are afraid to be in the same environment. The situation is so real that they fear it. It is real because the image is the reality. The image is the reality because one could be arrested, tortured for indeed having been a witness to your outburst and not having informed the police. In having witnessed and not reported it, they have become collaborators. The image is real because our only discourse with reality is through the image. And the nature of the discourse is real action. If the image is real, then our power over the image is just as real. We make it appear, we make it disappear, simply by pushing a button.

We make many creating/destroying actions repeatedly

through our use of the button. We play Chopin on our record player, the telephone rings, we turn the sound down, talk on the telephone, turn Chopin back up again. How normal it all seems. Within the last few decades of homo sapiens' existence, we have very quickly adjusted to button control. We use our powers over the button freely in an uncontrolled frenzy. We just push the button whenever and wherever we want to. There are no ethics, no aesthetics about the use of the button. One can just turn up Chopin, one can just turn him down. We control him. We use dictatorial powers over him in such a way that we ourselves don't realize their immensity and implication.

We use our power unfeelingly. We press buttons without feeling. We only know that when we press the button we will make things happen—the sound will be heard, the image will appear ("Let there be light."). We are not aware of our action as use of power, but merely regard it as a mechanical act. If we reflect on our behaviour we see an immense source of control that we never had in our existence, except through symbolic magic.

Being unconscious of the act has been characteristic of the destructiveness in us over the centuries. We have been most destructive with respect to both nature and civilization when we have not been aware of being so.

We wrote poems to the Industrial Revolution and the New Jerusalem. We wrote poems to ugly industrial cities, "Chicago hog butcher of the world, stacker of wheat" (Carl Sandburg). We wrote poems for exactly those things which we look upon today with disdain. We worship(ped), rationally of course, the Renaissance and the power of science. We claimed our species to be superior to all others and also saw it as our right that all our needs should be fulfilled at the cost of other life and the destruction of the planet. Everything for us. We are the greatest. We are supreme. The human is the most intelligent—having got rid of God it was even easier to make that claim.

III.

The distance between pressing a button to stop a Chopin symphony is not far from pressing a button and firing nuclear warheads. By having become accustomed to pushing buttons to achieve various ends we have become anaesthetized to the button. Pushing a button is very much part of us, like breathing and closing our eyelids. It is almost as if it were a part of our autonomic nervous system. We don't really think about pushing a button in the same way that we don't think about moving our feet when walking. The act of pressing the button over time seems to us to be independent of the result that it will produce. For the newly initiate to television or a telephone, it is magic to see and hear someone's voice from South America merely by punching a few buttons. But we get used to the act very quickly and eventually take it for granted. It is this state of taking the act, the mechanical act, for granted, of having become used to it, of having incorporated it into our behaviour as if the button were an extended appendage of our organism, that facilitates the use of the button for the annihilation of all life. With the button we have become amoral.

Human engineers have long been successfully applying the so-called science of ergonomics to fit man and machine together. The fit in some cases, especially in the use of war technology, has been so highly developed that man has become an extension of the machine, rather than vice versa. The original purpose behind ergonomics was that we should develop our tools in such a way that they would be in keeping with the physical characteristics of man – to make the perfect shovel so that with the least effort and back pain the farmer could do the utmost work; the most perfect dashboard on an automobile so that at a glance, without taking one's eyes off the road and causing a potentially fatal accident, the driver could know what was happening with his machine. That was supposedly the original idea — that machine would fit the needs of man, make life easier and safer for him.

Then, at one point, the machine became predominant. Life began to be thought and taught in terms of efficient systems, the thinking process in terms of flow systems. Cybernetics became a paradigm to explain human behaviour. Everyday vocabulary in language also began to change with mechanical terminology being used more and more frequently. Language became more machine-describing, machine-activity defining and qualifying, with less references to the whims and desires of man. Language became certain. It came to reflect a closed tight system.

We began to define our own behaviour in terms of efficiency. Learning machines were made to replace teachers. Biofeedback technology was developed for us to regulate the rhythms of our body. Time and motion studies of our behaviour in various settings ranging from the kitchen while cooking to the way we drive home after work were conducted. More and more, feelings were neglected, with random behaviour being considered an unhealthy aberration. Principles were lost in momentary detail; principles were lost in the partitioning of life activities into segments of specialization.

IV.

The push-button life has developed in this context —a context devoid of principle and feeling, a context of unquestioned action. A context in which we do not at all consider the consequences of our actions, which fit into the well-oiled, functioning, performing, action-oriented, goal-oriented society. We have no time for anything else but to go on, to always go on. For that we are applauded. For that we applaud ourselves.

There is no need to dwell on the video war games in which young people all over the world daily push buttons, killing aliens, enemies and monsters and also being killed, eaten up, mutilated by them. What is of interest is that the games are usually quite difficult to "win." That is the player often ends up getting killed. He keeps playing on, game after game, killing and forever getting killed. His motivation for continuing is having been killed, before having killed enough. If one could kill all the enemies in the first game, there would be little reason to play the simple game again. But that's not how the game is programmed.

Another aspect about pushing buttons that gives one a totalitarian control over life is that one can undo what one has done. By pressing buttons we can create words, images and formulas on a screen, which by the push of another button can be completely erased. Through buttons and screens nothing has permanence any more. We can even "create" art through techniques of holography as a here and now sensation. We can make it disappear as soon as we make it appear. There are also simulation exercises in which we can again experience various scenarios of the future simply by pressing buttons to activate various programmes.

Interactions that used to be carried out with other humans are now increasingly carried out as one-sided actions between the human and the button. The button has taken the place of the other human in what used to be a relationship. In some sense, it still is a relationship, as the same result is achieved. You press a button and get a coke, whereas before you used to ask for a coke to get one. Moreover, we now have machines that even say, "Thank you."

In another sense, however, it is not the same. The button is always under your command. It cannot refuse to serve you. A black man could be refused a coke by a white racist. With the new technology and the button replacing the other person, this is no longer possible. The black man will always get his coke.

Yet the button cannot protect us. The other person, especially your friendly neighbourhood grocer, could say, "You really shouldn't drink so much coke; the acid may not be good for your stomach. Why don't you try this apricot juice instead." The button can also not say "You look a bit worried today," or "Has something upset you?" The button cannot be concerned with you in the total context of your being. It can only react to a standardized and segmented part of your behaviour, treating it as an all or nothing activity.

V.

Because the button press behaviour abstracts all behaviour out of context, it takes away the possibility of any reaction from the environment. One cannot make an abominable request from a machine, because all requests are the same as far as the machine is concerned. In receiving no feedback from the environment one becomes more and more prone to one-directional thought. With no feedback, and with all requests satisfied through the machine, one becomes all powerful. Megalomania can set in. Witness the facial expressions of young people playing video games. They are in a never never land of their own, flying, soaring, killing monsters, killing aliens, killing enemies, killing, killing, killing.

With the button, the appearance of our activities has become more and more divorced, alienated from the essence.

We have come to the point in which the appearance (pressing the button) is the same, no matter what the essence (obtaining food, playing a symphony, making war) may be. We have come to the point where the appearance is now greater than the essence. The essence is only, if it is there at all, in the mind.

Once, food was grown, cut, gathered, cooked and finally brought before the family and eaten with prayers and full cognizance of the total experience. One knew and witnessed first-hand not only how the food had come, how it was prepared, but also to be thankful for it. In seeing the appearances (food in its various stages from field to table), one also knew very much the essence, being contiguous in the same mental context and physical space.

Once, one saw the making of musical instruments. One could even make a simple flute at home and play it. The instrument was played to the animals, to nature, to the gods and to each other. Skill, devotion and devoutness accompanied music and the players. When it was played (the appearance) it was not devoid of the essence. Once, there was a laundry day accompanied by its social folklore, interaction between women, exchanging stories, experiences. One tried to do a good job. Clothes were sorted, taken to the communal fountain, washed, carried back and hung to dry. Now the reality of the laundry is in the jingle of the advertisement for soap suds.

Once, one was raised to be a fighter, to be a warrior. He knew how to make and take care of his weapons. He learned how to handle himself as a warrior, which also meant a respect for life and most of all a respect for the enemy. The enemy was a person. One came face to face with the enemy and fought him to the death or captured him. The warrior had a sense of honour. One knew the reason for his fighting as did his mother, father, uncle, tribal chieftain, the gods, and wife and children. The fighting (appearance) was one with the person.

Now we can prepare food, play music, do our laundry and make war all in the same exact way—merely by pressing a button. The appearance (the act) is devoid of the essence (the act in its living context).

From the beginning of civilization until quite recently, the essence and the appearance were not so alienated. In some, especially rural societies today, they still are not. But with the condensing and miniaturization of life at the touch of a button, we could soon be automatons.

With the buttons, the essence, if at all, can only be in the mind. Some can imagine, having pressed the button, the missile taking off from its silo, travelling thousands of miles through space, reaching it's destination over a large city and then coming down, seeing the buildings, bridges, churches, parks, and finally the cars and the people – the bomb hits, explodes, the city is razed, another Hiroshima scene, burning skins, limbs scattered all over. This is the picture. It can only be mental, since we do not go with the bomb. We just press the button. The button-pressing usually prevents the above mental imagery. We think, as is our natural psychological inclination, not of the action that we have set in motion by pressing the button, but rather, of the next action, the next movement that we have to do. It may be pressing another button indicating that we have successfully pushed the first button as well. It may be punching in our code, our personal password, to confirm. It may be punching another button to get coffee and yet another to get a document. Whatever the case we go on with our motions in the context of our own physical and psychological space. Our mind does not follow our actions. We do not become one with the essence of the war act because it is so far removed from the immediate here and now appearance of reality.

Just pressing the button gives one a sense of accomplishment. It is an accomplishment easily achieved. It does not involve blood, sweat or tears. Just an emotion-void button press. Each day we keep on pressing more and more buttons. We get on and off buses by pressing a button. We press the button on the vibrator substituting for the penis the fire alarm, the phone to reach anyone almost anywhere immediately, the computer terminal for our work, and of course eventually the household robot. We have many buttons to push. We will have many more to push.

VI.

Seeing immediate results from immediate actions gives us a sense of control, a feeling of omnipotence. It is the feeling of importance that we as children attributed to our parents. It is the feeling of omnipotence that we once attributed to our mythological gods. With the button we have omnipotence on a daily basis. It is an omnipotence that however, has become pedestrian.

It is the poverty of omnipotence, for the button has replaced the dream and the myth. With children and especially with our gods, there was an awe, a wonder, a mystery with respect to the attributed omnipotence. Now there is no longer an attribution. The magic and the myth are gone. The button, based on science and technology, has become the primary cause. Our omnipotence is also in some senses impotent, as everyone can be god merely at the press of a button. And although we press the button, we are completely alienated from what happens inside the machine —knowing nothing of electrical currents, the Ohms law. It is we who press the button and make things happen. While making things happen we act in complete ignorance— ignorance of both the mechanics and the essence of the act. Totalitarianism is strengthened through ignorance.

The button makes us more and more ignorant. The button makes us more and more totalitarian. We have lost the essence of our actions and merely follow preordained behaviour patterns.

VII.

Taking photographs is yet another example of our actions leading to totalitarianism.

Our relationship with the camera manifests how the push button image is substituted for the real. With each relentless snapshot, all that is photographed is consumed, exhausted from its natural setting to become part of a series of unconnected images. The use of the camera is a theoretical mirror image of the use of the gun—the latter destroys by breaking up matter, the former destroys by abstracting matter from its context. More and more people are concerned with capturing the image and kidnapping the scene from its context, rather than becoming one, feeling, understanding, getting a sense of that which they are about to photograph. We in our century have become image consumers. We don't realize that one can never freeze a scene, seize a moment and record it.

We photograph relentlessly, attacking with our camera everything in the environment. When we know that taking photos may be offensive to someone, we unashamedly and in secret shoot from the hip. When we have our way, the camera clicks like a machine gun. As the soldier is alienated from his enemy in our century, so too is the photographer alienated from his subject. With each new visual experience we're trigger happy photographers. What is "new" for us, however, is always superficial. The novelty of the subject wears out almost as soon as it's photographed. Witness our behaviour with the camera as tourists, versus our non-use of the camera while at home. We are blind to that with which we are ultimately involved every day.

Each time we take a photograph, we destroy the sense of unity that the photographed object has with time and space. We abstract it out of its context. By the time the image reaches our photograph album (if at all), it is categorized and ordered in a new time and space context.

Parents take hundreds of snapshots of the new born bewildered baby exposed to one flash after another. With each day of his life he's photographed less, and finally, years go by without parents photographing their children.

No wonder Christianity was torn apart by the controversy over the prohibition of images. No wonder Islam is uncomfortable with images. Making, fixing images was considered to belong to the domain of god. With the first recorded images of man in cave painting some 35,000 years ago, image and magic were intertwined. The image had an all encompassing life giving presence, before which man was humble. In our century it is the image that is endlessly manipulated by man. The image is no longer lasting, being constantly created and destroyed. By ruling over images one rules over people. The image makers and the image destroyers are one and the same. They are the rulers.

Man had previously given such power only to gods. Now, it is a part of the everyday behaviour of the eight-year old child with a camera. Now, we have Kodak and Fuji Gods manipulated at will.

Our disrespect for life, our callousness with images enhances their totalitarian power over our perceptions.

VIII.

The "Scientific West" often looks down on the "Mystical East," in the sense that the East talks about fate, *kismet*, and a preordained life. It is now the button that has made life preordained. The process and results of all our actions are known in advance. Our choices are limited to the alternatives presented by the button. The result of pushing the button is guaranteed by the company manufacturing the product. Not only are our actions preordained but there is even a guarantee to go with it. We are not free. In our freedom to press the button we become a prisoner of the limitations of the machine. Our lives have become more and more mechanistic, more and more regulated, more and more subject to a thoughtless/emotionless routine. The seemingly infinite choices that time saving machines and push-button controls offer us are within very finite contexts. We are the subjects of our totalitarianism. Every time we press a button, the further we are removed from the act, as well as the meaning of our actions.

Zap! You're dead.

March 2, 1987, Marburg

HOMO SAPIENS BLUES

XVI

The Scream, Edward Munch, 1895

Then the Simiade broke off into two main branches. One, the Old World and the other, the New World Monkey. At a period much later, there broke off from the second branch the wonder of the universe, our most honoured human species.
Charles Darwin

I.

There are two schools in the West with respect to evolution —the "scientific" camp espousing Darwin's theories and the "religious" camp believing in creation.

Both the Darwinists and creationists hold something very much in common. Yet, we have long regarded the two views as diametrically opposed and mutually exclusive. Actually, they both support the same basic view with respect to the place of our species.

The creationists consider it an insult that we should be thought of in terms of having come from the apes, from being related to them. That has been the crux of the issue. We have a special place in the world and in the Heavens. We are created in the image of God. We are above all else. It is an insult to place us in the same plane as animals. In short, we are greater that all other forms of life.

For the Darwinists too we are at the zenith of evolution. We are the highest form of life on the evolutionary ladder. We are qualitatively different from other forms. We have language and our behaviour is learned, whereas the other forms depend mostly on species specific behaviour and genetically fixed action patterns. We can change our environment, whereas other forms can only adjust at best. In short, we are greater than all other forms of life.

The first belief rests with religion. The second, in the domain of the universities, the intellectuals, the "faithless," the Marxists. We follow one or the other.

Whether it is the evolutionary theory or the belief in creation, we reign supreme. We are the highest form of life on earth. In both belief systems, our position is unchallenged. Both belief systems base their views on a hierarchical order. In both belief systems life is not a juxtaposition of the organic and the inorganic. The earth, the solar system, the universe is not considered as an open, ever-changing evolving system with no rank orders and priorities. There is but little awareness of the process, the infinitely eternal movement that goes on and gives shape and shapelessness to matter and the cosmos. Nothing is more important than anything else. Though even the laws of entropy confirm both the interchangeability and the constancy of energy, we keep on ordering things. From the least to the most important, we categorize, we give priorities to all that is around us.

Like a general pinning a medal on himself, we too give ourselves a position above all others. Our concept of life is totalitarian.

II.

At the top of the hierarchy is the human. As we have put ourselves there, it is also up to us to remove ourselves, to do away with any notion of hierarchy. Yet in our vanity we seem to find it pleasing to enjoy this immense, sometimes conscious and sometimes unconscious power. It is also this power, this arrogance that spells at the same time a possible doom for the planet.

We worship our self-heralded place so much that even in so-called scientific research with respect to the capabilities of other species, and our attempts to find similarities between us and what we call the "lower" forms of life, we seek a reinforcement of our number-one place.

For years there have been projects trying to teach chimps, orangutans and gorillas human language. There has been "success." A female gorilla in California by the name of Koko is known to have signaled a male gorilla to climb on her back when she wanted to copulate. Rather than going on with instincts and feeling and letting the gorillas have their roll in the hay whenever they felt the urge without the necessity of words, we teach them, in the name of science, to have sex upon linguistic communication. Koko is now said to have developed human language to such a degree that she can communicate at the level of a four-year old homo sapiens child (i.e. functioning at Piaget's concrete operations level and using language to refer to the past, present and the future). But that, psychologists say, seems to be the limit. They can never reach our level. Similar experiments with dolphins, considered to be very intelligent, indicate that these animals too, cannot reach our level.

What do we mean by that? Intelligence in our image and on our terms!

Intelligence, as we, the homo sapiens, define intelligence!

III.

There is a greater order than that defined by our supremacy. We teach school children that one cannot subtract apples from oranges, then have our best scientists try to make humans out of apes. Why don't we try once to make apes out of humans? Perhaps then we can appreciate our arrogance and the almost infinite array of the combinations that exist with respect to sensing and perceiving the world. Each species senses and perceives the world reality in its particular way. We know how limited the sensations of homo sapiens is with respect to sight, touch, feeling and hearing. There may or may not be not be more than one reality, but there are certainly millions of different and not mutually exclusive ways of perceiving reality. Reality is a function of all those perceptions and sensations put together, communicated with each other.

Seeing ourselves at the pinnacle of development we make no effort to understand reality through other forms of life. Our only reason for studying them is perhaps to understand ourselves better. We experiment with animals, cut them up, do many unethical things (what would be unethical for us to do to each other) all for the purpose of serving the ends of homo sapiens.

For us to experience the perception of frogs, getting a sense of their world, would be no less a learning experience than observing the universe with a telescope. It is only when we see, hear and touch the cosmos through all other beings as well that we can get a fuller sense of life.

The aim of homo sapiens however, has not been to get a fuller sense of life, but rather to dominate life. Not only do we try to dominate each other, but all of us also dominate all other forms of life.

IV.

We began to worship ourselves, we began to write odes to ourselves with the Renaissance, the Age of Enlightenment and the Scientific and Industrial Revolutions. There was nothing that stood in our way. Not only were we capable of creating beauty, extolling the perfectness of the human figure, we were also able to explain the formerly divine mysteries of nature without heavenly guidance, but through scientific laws discovered by us.

We eventually began to write books not as humble servants of God, not for him, but rather began to dedicate them to our wives, mistresses, friends and children. With development in medicine we also began to have a greater power over life than ever before. It was due to our control over life that we have been able to increase the life span of our species by some forty years over the past few centuries. Now we reach for the stars and sometimes feel that nothing stands in our way. We have become so audacious in our beliefs and behaviour that a cosmonaut once made the following broadcast to earth from space, "I have been to the heavens and there is no God."

We now even have private profit-making companies who make and sell life. Not just the sperm banks and the test-tube baby technology, but also firms dealing with manufacturing and selling genes.

Man may be his own worst enemy but we feel there is also nothing greater. If there were to be no war, we say, imagine what all the power, all our genius, all our resources that we have not yet used would lead to. In peace, we shall be able to devote full energy to developing the world and space. We will eat better, be healthier, live longer (perhaps forever thanks to gene manufacturing and organ transplants), work less and perhaps come to a point where we don't have to work at all, with robots and machines doing all work for us. What better life can one envision? We will have created heaven on earth. A heaven which all can enter without having to wait in fear of God's decision on judgment day. Heaven on earth with man the supreme being.

Religions too, are for us to glorify ourselves in the name of God. If that were not the case religions would have talked about all living things and the harmony of life rather than holding us supreme. Man is so innocently supreme in the eyes of at least the religions of the book (Judaism, Christianity, Islam) that even his downfall is engineered by a snake.

Animals, plants, have no special place in the religious books. Why can't we also have raised an elephant from the dead, and performed miracles with blind dolphins and lame dogs? What lack of imagination stemming from our arrogance! Why don't cats perform miracles with kangaroos or ants with humans? Even miracles are in the domain of the homo sapiens. Any structural analysis of the books clearly shows the supremacy of our species over all other forms of life and "non-life."

V.

Whether one believes in evolution or creation, there is a commonly held notion that emotions are bad. Ethology, a science developed since Darwin, also supports both these views in the sense that of all the species, homo sapiens is the one least dependent on non-rational, instinctive behaviour. We deem, in the view of both systems of thought, instinctive behaviour as a lower, more primitive order of behaviour and say that it is through reason that civilization can progress. (What we mean by civilization and whether if indeed it progresses is, of course, open to question). Of all beings the human is the only one with the faculty of reason. Reason shall prevail. One should follow reason. It is through reason that we can advance. Civilization comes from the application of our reason. Reason over emotion prevents wars, murders, negligence. Reason is responsible. Emotions are wild, primitive. The distinction between the two (Apollonion/Dionysian) has existed for at least twenty-two centuries. Mind must prevail over body and reason over emotion. The scientific psychology of the human as developed by the 20th century hero Freud also posits the same. If the ego and the superego were not acting on the wild gratification seeking impulses of the id, not only would we have no order in society, but also no civilization, which according to Freud is the result of the libido (man's instinctive primitive hedonistic sexual energy) being displaced on to various other activities (creativity, governing, categorizing, collecting, etc.). Priests, psychologists, parents, law makers and rulers always appeal to one's reason over emotions. When something goes "wrong" in society, like a Hitler for instance, the explanation is simple. Hitler and Goebbels and Speer were masters in playing with the emotions of the people, engineering their feelings through symbols and demonstrations. Civilization, it is said, can only be reached with reason, and it is only homo sapiens who have reason. Non-reasonable activities in our species stem from the lower animal brain. With reason, we rule all totality totally. The rational individual is the zenith of totalitarian power.

VI.

In praising reason over emotion we have, as a species, allowed only one very specific exception—love. Never has one been heard to say in declaring love for another, "I am reasonably in love with you." The appeal to reason comes only when love is not there. Though reason and emotion are parts of an inseparable whole, by dividing the two, we have enabled one (reason) to rule over the other (emotion). We have created totalitarian dichotomies enabling us to divide and rule. One is madly in love ("I am crazy about you"), never intellectually. That, so far, has been the case in literature, song, theatre, opera, mythology. But now, the final triumph of reason over emotion in love has arrived with computer matching. We can now find our ideal partner through a scientific study of our character, interests and personality. Of course, the specialists of reason—psychologists, marriage counselors, social workers and contemporary priests who have studied the theories of psychological counseling—have also had a hand in this process. They have been able to say what is reasonably a good and what is reasonably a bad partnership or marriage. We can claim complete superiority. More and more we "love" rationally in order to protect our interests and personalities. With the victory of reason, we end love.

VII.

In explaining the development of civilization and the progress and accomplishments of humans, a very important stage is the domestication of animals. This is a half-truth. We speak only of one side of the story. We have domesticated only those animals that could have been domesticated—not the tigers, snakes and monkeys. The zebra would not be domesticated. The horse was. No one has even mentioned that the domestication of animals would not have been possible if they, the animals, had not instinctively co-operated. It is because fish always follow certain migratory patterns that we are able to catch them. If fish, chickens, horses and sheep were all created in such a way that they also exhibited dissonant activity (which is our main characteristic) changing and modifying their behaviour every which way—sometimes laying eggs every day and sometimes not laying eggs for months on end, if cattle choose not to eat and go on diets..! The point is that we are still completely dependent on the instinctive behaviour of animals for our survival. It is a result of having observed and understood the patterns of their instinctive behaviour that we have been able to domesticate them and feed ourselves. Only then could we have gone on with making cities, arts and wars. Civilization did not simply arise from the powers of our cerebral cortex. Without the instinctive behaviour of chickens and cows, life, as we know it today, would not have been possible.

Our capacity for change cannot be considered a quality until we become conscious of our actions and their effect, not only in terms of our species, but also in terms of all life. It is our ability to change that has put an end to the existence of many species already on earth. We have literally murdered one species after another. We have made species extinct. Yet, accustomed to our species' double standard, we have the gall to condemn genocide and speak out against capital punishment. Fine, but we should at least realize that these are the internal affairs of the species, of our species, and that the end of genocide and capital punishment is for the benefit of only our species. For lack of a better term, it is species-egoistic. It is egoistic because we abstract and exaggerate the value of our species above the value of all other life. We give trophies to hunters who kill other species while condemning to death those who kill their own.

VIII.

The evolutionists attempt to prove our supremacy by pointing out that the relative weight of the brain in proportion to the body is one of the greatest in the homo sapiens. They also point out that our brain has a highly developed cerebral cortex which is responsible for the "higher" faculties of thinking with most species having no cortex at all. What better scientific proof can there be to explain our supremacy?

Having the most developed brain means most developed in terms of certain characteristics like language and abstract reasoning. Other species also have certain parts of their brain, like the olfactory for smelling which are more developed, stronger and more sensitive than our brain. Some species have highly developed visual acuity. Thus, in that sense, it is not correct at all to say that we have the most developed brain; but at most we can point out specifically those activities particularly developed in the brain of homo sapiens. The term "most developed" implies that life and the universe have an all over purpose and that everything is gradually developing, evolving to best efficiently serve that purpose. The term also implies that the human, being most developed, is best suited to the serve the purpose of the universe!

In the general balance of things and harmony of the universe, there are no superior qualities, no superior functions of one species over the other. On the contrary, it is this concept of superiority that upsets the balance, interrupts the process from flowing in its rhythmic (though with ups and downs, point and counterpoint, harmony and dissonance) manner. Everything in life is a quality, every characteristic is a vital part of life and love. The process of evolution is dependent on the survival of a gene pool as heterogeneous as possible. That means each and every species is as vital as any other. Geneticists and biologists have usually referred to the gene pool in terms of homo sapiens. There is also the greater more universal gene pool of all species past and present, manifested both physically and psychologically in the interaction between the species. One cannot mix apples and oranges. But would not an apple be much less if there were no oranges?

IX.

We also have a very physical ideal of the perfect homo sapiens which has not changed over the centuries, at least not since the human form was idealized in ancient Greek statues in Praxiteles' ideal, beautiful body. Everything perfectly proportioned, everything perfectly functioning. He can run fast, throw the discus far, see over the horizon and listen to the fine tunes of the harp.

The post-Renaissance state is trying to create us all in the image of the Greek statue. But, like the ancient "civilized" Greeks, we no longer have to leave imperfect babies on mountain-tops to starve or be devoured by vultures. We can now, with the use of applied science, order the perfect and prevent the imperfect. We have the scientific knowledge and the technology to engineer our species. Through genetic control and manipulation we can prevent "defective" births and we can also even order, in the embryo, those characteristics that we want —at least sex in the immediate offing but eventually much much more choice will be available. We fear the "imperfect" person, we pity him, we have sympathy for him, we look down upon him, we feel uneasy because of him. In our image of the perfect person, he is inferior. In being of "sound mind and body," we see ourselves closer to the ideal of the perfect. There are some of us who indeed think that they would be perfect if it weren't for that one pimple. Not only are we, the homo sapiens, at the top of the hierarchy of all life, but there is also a hierarchy within our species.

The hierarchy is based on the notion of those who are lower, those we call the physically handicapped—the blind, the deaf, those without limbs. In our humanitarian scientific efforts, if we cannot prevent their birth, we try to make them as perfect as possible. We try to save them. The value system that we attach to their physical characteristics is that of our superiority and their inferiority.

They are also made to feel inferior because of their physical handicaps. This is nonsense. It is a totalitarian imposition of a value system. True, that they lack a particular sense or organ, but it is just as true that what they lack in one organ they compensate for in others. There is no question that the so-called handicapped develop a certain special extraordinary relationship between their other senses, that we perhaps cannot even dream of.

Yet, in our totalitarian value system of the perfect person, we encourage them to be like us. We encourage them to emulate our talents and skills based on the particular juxtaposition of our five senses. We encourage them to play the same sports. We even encourage them to participate in an absurd event based on our reality—Olympics for the handicapped!

In trying to model them after us, in their trying to model themselves after us, we again reinforce the totalitarian structure of the subjugator and the subjugated, the colonizer and the colonized upon which both psychological and physical power in society is distributed. Being imprisoned in such a value system of classifying and categorizing, the so-called physically handicapped lose all their unique potential, their creativity, their chance to explode in their particular richness and set new vistas and models for behaviour and thought for all of us. By subjugating them to our image of the perfect, we all lose the opportunity to enhance our perception of reality. We prevent the enrichment of our lives and the chance to share more of the richness and the mystery of life. But we may be losing even more than that. Such physical differences, what we call physical handicaps, are perhaps, or will one day, be very necessary for the survival of the species and even of the planet.

I remember a class that I was "teaching" on individual differences at Boğaziçi University in Istanbul, expounding to the students that one never knows when a particular characteristic, looked upon disfavourably and as a handicap in one context, might be vitally necessary in another. As an example I referred to blindness, speculating that perhaps all of us, all of a sudden, might be exposed to such a radiation that we would all go blind. If there were no persons in society who were already blind and thus knew their way about, everything might just collapse. It would be on the basis of the ability of the blind "to see" in this new context that we would be able to go on. The record of our history, literature, music would also be available only to them in Braille. In the new order we would be dependent on the blind rather than they on us (though it would be just as totalitarian since all forms of dependence are totalitarian). There was a blind boy in class, Emin, who said nothing. Some months later we were on the Aegean coast near Halicarnassus (Bodrum) and swam into a cave by the sea with my former students including Emin. We ventured in a bit far, had no more light, could not see anything, lost our sense of direction. The distance between the ceiling of the cave and the water level became ever less. It was then that Emin assumed a position at the head of the group (from what I could tell by his voice) and laughing, joking and singing, he led us out of the sea cave and into brightness.

This example should not be taken to mean that we should not use available knowledge and technology to restore sight to the blind and limbs to the so-called handicapped. Contrarily, it also does not mean that we should design such a system of genetic engineering that we should allow for all sorts of variety for all foreseeable situations. It would be an impossible and a mad project with man playing god again.

The point is that there is a great distance, a mental psychological distance between the physical state of a person and our attitude toward him. The attitude does not correspond with reality. It only reflects the totalitarian order we impose on ourselves and nature.

Emin, in his state, is just as beautiful and just as necessary for the species as everyone else is. No one is superior. We all indeed need each other. Until we get rid of this notion of superiority and hierarchy we threaten our own survival. Dissonance and conflict come from a hierarchic model. Cooperation and harmony come from a world view which seeks not the order of things but rather the uniqueness of everything. Dissonance and conflict bring destruction. Cooperation and harmony bring creation. There is conflict in creation as well. But, the conflict is between the individual and his infinite search to hear, see, touch, feel and love, rather than collecting and categorizing experiences.

X.

We are totalitarian because our understanding of life as a species is built on power and domination and not on love and harmony. We have power over other species. We domesticate animals. We put them in circuses and zoos. We bring plants to botanical gardens, plants and animals to our homes. We can become masters of all life in our very homes, teaching dogs tricks, making cats chase pieces of string, watching hamsters in perpetual motion. All this gives us an immense source of power. We are the dominators. We feed our subjects. They are dependent on us for their lives. We play with them whenever we want. We pet them whenever we want. We love them when we want and push them away when we don't. We even decide to have them "put to sleep" when we want. We decide to castrate and sterilize them.

We, the homo sapiens, even in our very homes, every day, together with our children, ruthlessly rule over all the other species.

In the U.S., as in many other countries, old and lonely people are placed in old people's homes to wait their death. They are alone. Yet, they need to love. As with people in all institutions they do not love each other. In fact, many refuse to speak with each other, are very selfish, bitter, aggressive. Solution—give them something to love. What? Simple! There is an organization that once a week, for a couple of hours a day, brings cats and dogs to these people so that they can pet them. Animals, like a travelling brothel, are transported from home to home, from person to person.

Imagine if you and I were sent from house to house to be petted. This is done in the name of love and tenderness.

It is done for humanity. Specifically because humanity is only concerned with, as the word clearly suggests, humans. Humanity means love of the human. It does not concern itself with other forms of life. The means again justifies the end. For the sake of humanity we pay no respect, no attention to other forms of life.

We will not be able to have peace on earth until we become conscious of the fact that we at present have no peace with life on earth. We are engaged in a totalitarian war of domination and destruction against all other species on earth. We are as aware of our totalitarianism as we are aware that we breathe.

XI.

Evolution has not stopped. It is forever taking place through natural selection and mutations and perhaps also other processes of which we are not aware.

To place homo sapiens at the top of the evolutionary hierarchy contradicts the very nature, the very process, the very definition of evolution. Who is to say that a new species with greater adaptability to the environment will not evolve? We have an ethnocentric, species-centric theory of evolution which stops with us as if evolution had a purpose and its ultimate purpose was the creation of our species.

Creation has not stopped. The universe is forever expanding into the darkness of the cosmos, into infinity. The finite universe is expanding into infinity. What is happening? What is evolving? What about parallel universes? We haven't the faintest! From the point of view of the future, man may not only have a different place in evolution, but may also think of evolution in a totally different paradigm.

It is the processes of creation and evolution that are remarkable and not particularly the species. Species come and species go. Over 90% of all species that once existed are now extinct. But the process goes on, life goes on. We are still on the very primitive level of thinking about the course of our individual life and its possible aftermath. If on another level of consciousness we thought in terms of the life of the species or in terms of the universe (though individually we may become less significant in our own eyes), we would become more with life and the universe. Just consider that, like our birth, the solar system also had a beginning, only four and a half billion years ago. Consider that the earth and Venus will collapse into our sun as it is blacking out, dying only 5000 million years from now.

We are part of a process that goes on and on. We are not the end point of evolution or creation frozen in time. We have had our coming, we will also have our passing. We are not a result. We are not an end. We are not building up to something grander, stronger, more beautiful. We do not have a goal. We are not predestined. We are just part of an ever-changing process. There is no immortality—neither of the individual, the species, the world, the sun, the solar system, or the galaxy. Things coalesce, have seemingly a beginning, take form, then disappear only for new forms somewhere else to appear in an ever-changing inter-active process.

XII.

The more we impose our predominance in our mental sets with respect to our concepts of immortality and the central place of the human, the less we see and understand of life and non-life. In order to comprehend life it is first non-life that we must appreciate. We don't have the consciousness of the bright universe floating only as a speck of light in the infinite darkness of the cosmos. Our consciousness is ordered in such a way as to place ourselves way up on top of the pinnacle.

Only some hundred years ago, before the Copernican Revolution, we thought and believed that the earth was at the centre of the universe, that the sun and everything else circled around the earth. We think that silly now, attribute it to our ignorance and the anti-scientific tradition of the church. We blame societal structure for our ignorance. We do not blame ourselves. We ignore our particularly peculiar characteristic of worshipping ourselves, of attaching importance to ourselves. Of course, at the basis of our self-importance is our insecurity as a species. We don't know anything about anything in spite of the fact that we can observe, ask questions and even predict things like eclipses and the coming of Halley's Comet. We are curious but we are also very much scared of the unknown.

The result is that, like a bunch of sheep scared by a wolf, we flock together within the context of a particular species consciousness. We block out, repress, suppress certain questions about the unknown and feel comfort in reaffirming our importance. The species megalomania gives us strength to avoid fear. It gives us a false sense of strength thereby preventing an inferiority complex of the homo sapiens. We do not see ourselves in the perspective of higher orders of consciousness.

We, as homo sapiens, have no empathy for the other. We are so presumptuous, so totalitarian, that we refuse to recognize other species on an "equal" basis. Just like the white Europeans who refused until recently the black African as really a member of our species. We have put ourselves on a pedestal.

We think of ourselves as unique, original, incomparable. We have given ourselves a special place in the order of things. The central importance that we give to the homo sapiens is no less ludicrous than the central place that we gave to earth a few hundred years ago. We have, on the basis of undeniable physical evidence, know the Copernican Revolution to be fact. But 500 years on, we have not made the psychological revolution. Our world view still does not conform with the facts as we know them. Although we know that the earth is no longer at the centre, psychologically we are still at the centre of the universe. Our religions only deal with the story of homo sapiens. In spite of the awareness of new facts which have radically changed our place in the cosmos, we still formulate our psychological superstructure, our perception of the I and the not I, on the basis of the view and place of man as it was thousands of years ago.

Our species consciousness does not correspond to reality. It is, in clinical psychology terms, pathological. We refuse to see reality. Yet we know the new reality. We repeat it in school—the existence of quarks, electromagnetic energy, the quantum theory and the uncertainty principle of Heisenberg, the existence of dark and anti-matter and dark energy. Yet we seem to have made a contradictory but compatible dichotomy between our factual scientific world universe consciousness and our species consciousness. In this sense, we seem to be schizoid, with a split personality.

We parrot the facts of the universe and the age of the solar system. It goes in one ear and out the other. The new information is like rote learning. It does not mean anything to us. How many of us know the age of homo sapiens—our very own species? How many of us even know the age of the earth, the moon, the sun? Yet we attach so much significance to individual birthdays, wedding anniversaries, national holidays. There are dates that are never forgotten in our over-exaggerated pathological attention to our rites. Example: In Turkey every year on the 10th of November, at five past the hour of nine in the morning, whistles and sirens sound all over the country. All traffic stops. People in their homes stand up and come to attention. Everything stops for one minute. Seventy million people stop so that they can commemorate the exact moment that the founding father of the country, Mustafa Kemal Atatürk, died on November 1Oth, 1938. Now, this is not, please, a particular genetic-cultural pathology of the Turks. We all go to endless trouble all over the world in glorifying ourselves on the basis of certain dates—we either suffer, celebrate or fast. Dates are very much a part of our thought/ emotion paradigm. The chance of us dying on our birthday, for instance, is more than any other day.

If the dates are not respected, remembered, scandals and catastrophes can ensue. We know so much about our individual, nation-state or religious days, yet we have little knowledge and no emotional or cognitive attachment to dates that have something to do with the very core of our existence. Our self-adulation comes as a result of our suppressing our past and present in the universe. We have no life consciousness of the reality that we factually know.

XIII.

Neither religion nor science have the same hold over us as they once did. They no longer rule the day. We no longer think of tomorrow. "Apres moi, le deluge" is the basis of our relationship with each other, ourselves and the planet. Our species is perceiving itself as if in a void, as if in a vacuum. We have built a species-centric world order like an ostrich burying his head in the sand.

Our totalitarianism is in the exaggeration of our species, in the megalomania of the species to see itself as both the possible creator of all beauty and destruction. We are neither many nor mighty. And the earth is but a minute speck in the cosmos, not even as large as a mosquito.

We are totalitarian because we see nothing comparable to us. We are over and above everything else on earth and in the universe. In our minds we dominate the past, present, and even the future. Science-fiction is no more than a rationalization and justification of the importance of our species. We emasculate, we castrate, we anthropomorphize the mystery of space.

Our art forms dealing with the cosmos are homo sapiens-centric. In science-fiction the enemy, the alien, only appears to be mysterious. There are elements of danger in dealing with him. But in the end, homo sapiens prevails. The mystery is understood. The films *2001*, *Solaris, Close Encounters of the Third Kind*, and *Matrix* could have opened new doors to humble us, to move us away from our homo sapiens-centricism. Instead, we have gone in the opposite direction. The image of ourselves today also rules over tomorrow.

Chained by our self-appointed supremacy, we rule over all beings, all things, all time. It is only the rulers who can liberate themselves from ruling. Let us first liberate ourselves from tomorrow. Perhaps we can all begin with science fiction. We can begin by visualizing a future in which homo sapiens do not rule.

March 18, 1987, Marburg

WHY CHILDREN?

XVII

Delicate balance, 1998
Terry Winn

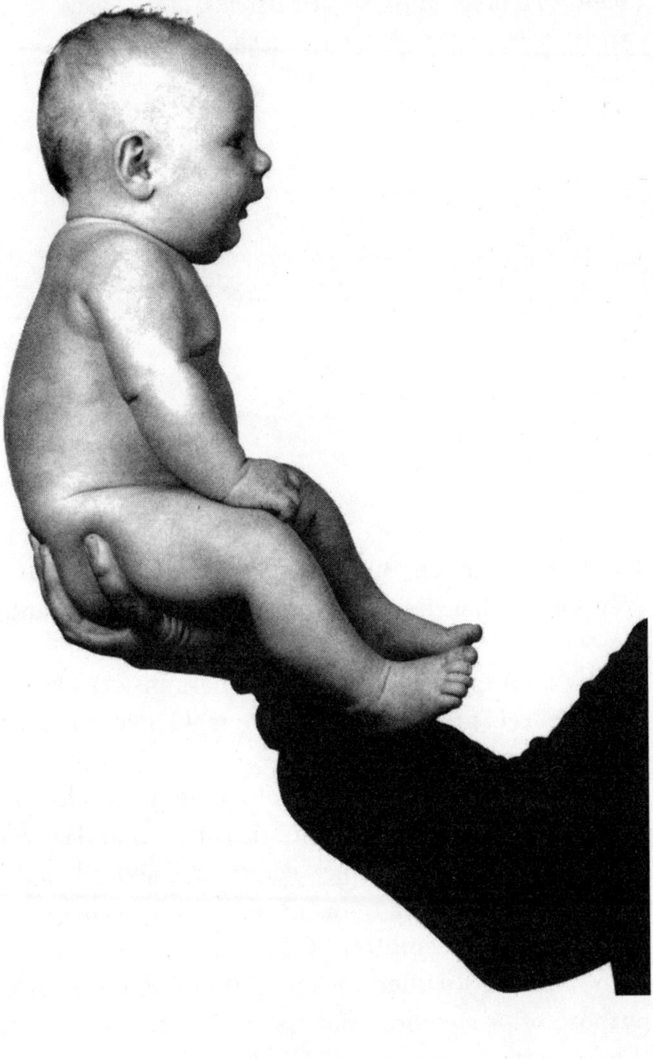

Children begin life by liking their parents; in time they criticize them and rarely forgive them.
Oscar Wilde

I.

The Pope today encouraged married people to have children saying that they should participate in the "banquet of life."

Why do we make children? The best answer I've heard is that one feels incomplete until we make two, three or even four children and more.

I've heard many other answers. One has to do with immortality. I will die but live through my child. Having children is also effected by one's social class and religion. Peasants, who need as many hands as possible to help with the land, have many children. Catholics also have many children because, for them, it's a sin to have sex without the purpose of procreation. But this evades the basic question. Why one has so many children is one thing, why we have children at all is another.

II.

The expressions "OUR child," "To HAVE" children are manifestations of our inclination to possess. What right have we to HAVE children? What right have we to pass on to them our religions, our expectations, our rewards and punishments? What right have we to be their masters, as if they were slaves, rather than be simply their loving caretakers?

III.

The most fundamental reason why we have children is because we can. In fact, we as a species venture to do most things simply because we can. Even suicide! Simply because we are capable. That is the story of our species. We test our limits. We try to go beyond our limits.

But... is that any reason to have children? Just because we can? This, in spite of the fact that as a species we can reason.

Yet with the exception of some religious orders who bind themselves to celibacy, we go on and on in sowing our seed with little thought. Even in the face of starvation and war, our history is filled with examples of continuing to procreate. If there is an exception to this it is only to choose the time that is right for us.

IV.

We have children because others do.

We have children because our parents want and expect us to.

We rarely have children for the sake of the child to be. Having children has less to do with the child than anything else. Grandparents, prophets, neighbours, school buddies steadfastly prompt us to have children. The child to be, exists not in and of itself but in the image of others. The bond to the child evolves only during the pregnancy. Only after it becomes an extension of ourselves rather than a being on its own. We only begin to have an inkling that there is to be another being, an individual, after the fact. Only after the child announces its presence.

V.

If we are honest with ourselves, we can list thousands of other reasons why the child is not wanted for its own sake. Among the most abominable is inheritance. We have children to keep our wealth from going to someone else. Although one is rarely inclined to share one's possessions, it should at least go to our offspring, we say.

We have children because we want to hold on to our partner. Think of those who have children with the idea of just holding on to their partner. Having children as blackmail. Having children just to make separation difficult, less probable.

There are those who make children because of the benefits that they may get from governments, social security systems and various other agencies.

Many of us have children out of jealousy. Those with children look upon themselves as if they're in some way superior. They make others feel that in some way they just haven't made it.

We have children to prove to ourselves that we are fertile males and females.

In the thousand and one ways in which we decide to have children, the child rarely enters the picture.

How many of us make children as proof of our love for each other? Don't we want to realize that the "each other," that "You" and "I" have nothing to do with the child? The love for each other may make us better parents (and that only if our love is not so selfish as to be to the detriment of the child) but we don't GIVE a child to each other as if exchanging gifts on Valentine's Day. The child should be the subject of love, not the object of our love for each other.

VI.

Those who seek freedom for the sake of their own desire to rule, even if it is to rule over themselves, violate the most fundamental freedom by projecting their own totalitarian desires. So do those who have children, not because they want them, but because the child fulfills a certain need. In such cases the child is used. To use and exploit others is indeed totalitarian. But to create a child not for its own sake but for another reason, is the epitome of totalitarianism in our species.

VII.

Child-bearing is an all or nothing act. After one's wealth disappears, after one's partner disappears, after we have proven our fertility, after we have set the stage for our immortality, after we are no longer jealous of those with children, the child is still there! A product of needs that no longer exist. A product of needs that have been met through the child, with the living child as the reminder. As that which has been left over.

VIII.

When the child is created out of needs that have nothing to do with the child it can become a potential nuisance. A sacrifice for the parents. A radical alteration of life styles for the sake of the child. The sexual, social, professional, leisure life of the parents is altered in ways not often welcome.

With the birth of the child, not created for its own sake, also begin the demands of the creators. I say creators, for in their arrogance, the parents look upon themselves as the creators of the child. As if creation could be so simple an act as the result of a few minutes of male-female copulation.

The parents rarely let the child develop in its own freedom. They usually model their child in accordance with the standards of contemporary society and their particular whims and desires.

IX.

The process of maturation, the growing up of the child, is often referred to as passing from a state of dependence to independence. Like the young of all other animals, so too with the human child. Once it becomes independent and can fend for itself, it leaves the nest, the home. But one can also make the opposite argument. The process of growing up in the human child is also the process of losing one's uniqueness and independence of spirit. The child growing up is like a wild horse being tamed, domesticated.

This is more than just socialization, learning the do's and don'ts of society. It is also an aesthetic and cognitive conditioning. It is an imposition of perceptual patterns from an infinite array of possibilities. With respect to the development of all his senses the child is conditioned by immediate contemporary society.

(S)he is not given the opportunity to have a sense of the perceptual and cognitive patterns of different civilizations across history or other concurrent cultures. The parents, though possibly inclined to move in and out of different cultures and tastes, and certainly with at least an awareness of them, most often enclose the child within a particular field, thereby not addressing his flexibility or fulfilling his potential to create his own connections and culture.

X.

Child bearing and the parent-child relationship can be non-totalitarian under one condition: through the awareness of the miracle of life, the uniqueness of life. For whatever reasons the child may have been conceived, it is only enough for us to realize that, that which has been created has little to do with us.

It's as independent of us as a cloud in the sky, a butterfly, the change of seasons.

It is as much a miracle as all others. It falls to us to nurture the child, but not to order it. It falls to us to observe the miracle and let it develop individually just as does the body develop its organs, limbs, eyes and ears without our interference, but with concern.

Unfortunately, our totalitarian control is extending in the opposite direction. Not only have we established control over the "spiritual child" over the centuries, we are now, also seeking ways to control and eventually design the genetic development and attributes of the child. Should it become utilitarian in the future, there is no reason for us not to create a human with eyes that can rotate 360 degrees, with two heads waking and sleeping in turns.

With the way things are going, it's not difficult to imagine children made-to-order, and boutiques designing children in accordance with the spirit and needs of the time. But then, as we enter the age of all of us becoming cyborgs, children's liberation will eventually come through their being able to act on who they are and how they are. Children are our last slaves.

March 9, 1988, Kea

THIS MAGIC MOMENT

XVIII

Titania and Bottom, Henry Fuser, 1790
(*Midsummer Night's Dream*, William Shakespeare)

I am not here.
Orhan Pamuk

I.

You wait for that one second. That one instant in your life that you have been wanting, preparing for.

Man lands on the moon, "This is a small step for man, a giant stride for mankind," says the astronaut as he sets foot.

You win the gold medal in the Olympics. Tears come into your eyes as the national anthem is played.

You make love.

You see Venice for the first time.

We are not an instant.

You cannot prepare death.

You cannot prepare life.

They come as they are.

You cannot abstract a moment out of life. Nothing can depend on the moment. Everything is a part of the process.

We cannot take moments out of past processes and build a case of past happiness or past dread.

Anything reconstructed, based on recollections of past moments is a prison. It is a fortress keeping out life.

We cannot build the future on the expectation of moments, images, visages.

We are all part of a process, indeterminately determinate. We go. Sometimes we flow. Sometimes we swim against the tide. Sometimes we persist and drown. Sometimes we tire and leave the water.

Go, not with persistence, but with life. Then, whether we drown or flow on does not matter. For all is life.

Except, to leave the water.

For the water is never left. There is never a shore.

The only shore is suicide.

Is that life?

Is that also not freezing a moment?

All that life –the past, the present and the future– all frozen in that one instant of the act of suicide.

Why?

Because the moment is exaggerated. Because the moment has a totalitarian influence on the determination of life.

II.

There are no moments. There is (no) time. There is life eternally fleeting. It goes on and on and on and on. Life goes on. We go on. Something always has and something always will go on. The moment stops life. It freezes life. One should hear the birds in the forest without having to stop. One should hear the roar of the ocean without having to stop.

Make love. Without comments. Without reservations. Kiss without immortalizing the moment. Go, go and go. Never stop for the moment. With the moment we go back in time. Freezing the present we escape into the past. Freezing the present moment, we become part of the past. Flow with time.

Do not wait for the next moment. There is no next moment. There is no next. It goes on and on. Be with the moment. Be with every moment.

No moment is as it should be. No moment is as it would have been. No moment is as should have been. We cannot order moments. We cannot order time. We cannot order lives. Ours or anyone else's.

There is no difference between our life and their life, between my life and yours. We are all in the same life. We are all with each other.

No moment **should** have been a happy one. One cannot order a happy moment. Not from the past. Not from the future.

It is not a tragedy that one dies on the way to the wedding. There are no tragedies. Tragedies come from our expectations and orderings of life. Tragedy is the result of the totalitarian expectation. Tragedy is a totalitarian force.

In expecting, in thinking that we deserve, in believing that we are entitled to certain moments in life, we become totalitarian.

Then what joy is there when what we expect happens? When what happens is what has been foretold, wanted, expected? What joy is there in ordering? And when it doesn't happen (as it usually does not) what reason is there to curse fate, curse yourself, curse this or that? Wish that you hadn't been born. Wish that God would help you. Wish that, that, that, that and that... When it doesn't happen, when the moment is not as expected, it is a disappointment. It does not mean however, that nothing has happened.

III.

For those so-called all important momentous decisions we ponder and ponder. We consult friends, we ask the wise. We look for hints from symbols. Try coffee fortunes, tarot cards. We vacillate from one position to another. Yet, it often comes to pass that a decision was not necessary. Or, the decision had already been made by others. Sometimes we just can't make a decision, and sometimes, not deciding one way or the other, we choose a middle way, a safe way. Sometimes, we make the momentous decision only to make a contrary one later.

It is totalitarian to think that we have ordered our lives. Not only do we have the false notion that we think that we order life, but we also have the presumptuousness to order joy, to plan the perfect setting for ourselves. All these things that we want OUT of life. Why is the expression not all those things that we want IN life? Why out of life? Why from life? Because we abstract moments. We try to create our lives in a vacuum. In the abstract. In absentia of life. And whenever the life "out there" intervenes –shows itself– we curse our fate.

When that, which we have been planning for happens, we think that we have created that situation. We take credit for what has happened. What has happened is not necessarily what was expected. We can will what we wish we never had.

Who does what to whom, how, when, and where, we do not know. We can make plans but we cannot possess life. Making plans and having the plans come true should not reinforce a feeling that we are in control of our lives. We are not. No one is. There is no fate. No *kismet.* No one is in control.

The process flows, forming and being formed. There is no control of moments. The notion of control gives us security. But the same notion also leads to our not being one with life.

There are no especially beautiful or sad days in life. It is the order that we impose that makes the day beautiful or sad. Each day is as equally beautiful as it is sad.

It is in taking life as it is that we become one with it. Then, we are in harmony. There is a harmony to happiness just as there is to sadness. It is the harmony that is the essence. Not the moment of happiness or sadness.

IV.

The construction of the moment—the expectation of the moment is totalitarianism. It is the moment of death. In our expectancy we kill life. In our expectancy we kill ourselves. We kill because things have not happened as we wished.

What do we kill because it has not happened as we wished?

We kill our children because they have not turned out as we wanted them. A boy instead of a girl. A child when least expected. We kill them in the image of the expected moment. We kill them for the sake of our expectation. Why do people have children? For many reasons. Because they think that they will be happy? Happiness is having a child. No! One who is not happy without a child cannot be happy with a child. One has no right to claim happiness on the basis of another. It is only (s)he, who recognizes happiness everywhere, can also be happy with a child. Together in happiness. Not happiness from.

How many fathers have forced sons and even daughters to mold them in their own image? And how many sons and daughters have failed their parents because they could not fit that image? How many sons and daughters have lived for years, all their lives, trying to fit that image? Rebelling against fitting that image? But in either case always living with the frustration and guilt of not having been one with that image. Life long we try either to fulfill or rebel against expectations. Enough! There is life. Life is before all expectancy. It is above all and one with us. We are one with it.

We demean life because we try to order it. We kill life because we think we can order it.

No, we cannot. But we can be open to life. Open to our thought/emotions about life. We might always still be disappointed with ourselves and our species. But let us live fully the thoughts and emotions that come with living life. Let them not be held in check by the thoughts and emotions that we have with respect to our expectations about life.

We are often involved in a conflict between our expectations and what life brings or can bring. How often we say, "I'd love to do that but I have not time".

Time is relative. We have all the time in world and we have no time at all.

We are daily in the process of trying to build and support structures that keep our expectations in the forefront. It is said that it is those expectations that give one personality, determination, chance to realize one's potential.

Get lost in the moment. Live the moment. But do not seize the time. Be one with time, in time and outside of it at the same instant.

We make a circus of magic moments in our lives. Our lives are a series of events with the hope that each event will lead to a magic moment.

We make magic-moment ceremonies. Magic-moment rituals. The birth is a magic moment ceremony. American fathers pass out cigars (death smoke at birth). The church baptizes. The birth is a magic moment. You have to do something to celebrate the magic moment. If you do not, if something goes wrong with the celebration, everyone and especially you are let down. Is it a bad omen?

Wedding is a magic-moment ceremony. The first night with husband and wife, two lovers, is a magic-moment ceremony. We have expectations of these magic-moment ceremonies. They have to be just right. It has to be so right that we even rehearse for the magic-moment ceremonies. Wedding rehearsals in churches!

First day in school is a magic moment. Graduation is a magic moment. Death is a magic moment. All magic moments bring pressure. All magic moments are oppressive. Even in their joy they are oppressive. For they have been rehearsed. We await the magic moment with the expectation that at that moment we will be happy. At that moment all worries will cease. At that moment life will begin anew. The magic moment is regarded as a new start in life. In our minds we have a definite picture of what we will be like in the magic moment. We daydream for years about the magic moment. The prospective bride, from the age of whatever on, thinks of the day of her wedding, her husband, the prince on a white horse.

We make future magic-moment images which, while orienting us to a point up the road of life somewhere, also let a lifetime slip away. In waiting for moments we lose our hold on life. In waiting for moments we become blind to life.

V.

Power structures in society receive their strength and legitimacy from the magic moment. At the top comes religion. The religious hierarchy needs the magic moment to affirm its power, to affirm its control over the people. It is only with the blessing of religion that one can live the magic moment. Birth, initiation, marriage, death,—all the key magic moments of life on earth— are lived, carried out under the auspices and control of religion.

There is also an industry that thrives on the magic moment. Food caterers, tuxedo renters, doctors, musicians, priests, earn a living, make profits from the magic moment.

The dominant forces and structures and social institutions receive their power from us, from our unfilled yearning to seek magic moments.

Psychologists and psychiatrists promise their clients/patients the strength, to once more seek their magic moments.

With each new ideology, revolution and regime in history, we expect the sum total of our magic moments to be fulfilled with utopias. We have the feeling that with this regime (French, Soviet, Islamic Revolutions) everything is possible, that we start anew. That life is fresh. That now, we all have our moment.

What we have is only the moment of the victory celebration (which may last from a day to a few months). Revolutionary regimes always talk about the long road to progress and the need to sacrifice, while always reminding us of the magic moment that once was. Through heroes, songs, tales of the revolution year after year, we relive the past magic moment.

The past revolution, the new totalitarian power, justifies its existence on the basis of the magic moment.

VI.

Our first account of time, our first calendars were used to help understand the passing of months and seasons so that we knew about the tides and floods. When to plant, when to store supplies for the winter, when to expect again the warmth of the summer. Across centuries we developed evermore sensitive instruments to measure the passing of time, until today when we are even aware of the second hand on the watch. In quantifying time to it's elements of the day, hour, and minute, we try to order and rule over our daily lives. But whereas, at first. we observed the rhythms of nature, we now use our watches to keep a watch over us. It is with watches and clocks that we determine when we wake, eat and sleep. More and more we eat lunch not because we are hungry but because it's twelve; more and more we sleep not because we're sleepy but because it's late; more and more we wake up to an alarm. Yes an alarm (!), rather than naturally. We order our lives according to watches, according to hours and minutes.

We have become prisoners of our own time-keeping system. It is from the confines of this prison that we have created the myth of the magic moment. The magic moment is the antithesis of each passing moment that permeates our lives. Freedom comes from the sense of eternity, from not being bound to time, from not being a prisoner of the moment, from not awaiting the illusive magic moment of the saviour.

It is in our timelessness that we can sense our freedom.

March 24, 1987, Marburg

THE TOTALITARIANISM OF LOVE
(As Practiced)
XIX

Man's Head in Women's Hair, Edward Munch, 1906

I love you.
Anonymous

I.

"I can't live without you" is a statement offering oneself to be possessed and ruled by the other. The same person may believe in democracy, independence, self-growth. Yet, in love, one often succumbs to the opposite. One posseses and is possessed.

Our expressions of love lead to a state of domination over each other and more. We place our particular love above all else. We let it dominate our work, relations with others, life style, value system. Life, in the name of love, is turned upside down.

It is precisely because of this total submission that love does not last. With the possession of love, love ends. "I can't live without you," becomes a cry of despair from the one left behind. In between the beginning and the end, expressions and gestures from the pre-possession stage continue, albeit with less sincerity and intensity, until the inevitable end.

There is no reason why love should be consumed so quickly or even consumed at all. It is our concept of love, our attitude toward each other as ordered by the specific language and customs of our way of loving that should be questioned. We have put such a uniform on love, we have defined love in such a totalitarian way, that the state of being in love is often of short duration, subject more to the way we define love than to our feeling-thoughts and thought-feelings.

II.

Possessed love ends quickly. It ends because we seek freedom. Love, as defined, as it has been defined from at least the time of Sumerian and ancient Egyptian poetry until present day is against freedom. Across centuries, there has been a contradiction between the practice and definition of love and our expectations.

An ancient Persian metaphor looks at love as a cage which those on the outside want to enter, and those inside want to escape.

Once the initial period of possessed love is over, most relationships survive through a process of incremental freedom and avoidance, contradicting all that had been said while "in love."

Such changes are detrimental to self-esteem. Many get depressed, repress their thoughts. Many, in the light of others' experience, see their new situation as a fact of life to which one must resign oneself. Some, because they cannot face double standards, leave their partner, only perhaps to fall in love again, and once more go through the same cycle.

Some couples have open relationships proving their independence while trampling on the feelings of all others. All this because, usually because, we are defining love in such a way that it has little to do with love.

III.

It is not love or its brevity that we should question but our definition of love. In songs, poetry, art, i.e. all depictions of love in history. It is these that should be questioned.

"I'm crazy about you."

No!

Love is not an abandonment of the self to the so-called irrationality of the emotions. Love is not the emotions dominating the mind. There is no domination. The centuries old dualism of mind versus the emotions is not correct. It is not in keeping with the reality of who we are. Emotions and thoughts are together, entwined with each other. There are thought-emotions and emotion-thoughts.

With the "love is irrational" model, we have long adhered to a structure that has led to a withering of love. That love is irrational, that one falls madly in love, has been our model. Indeed, when we fall in love, we fall madly in love. We are crazy about the other person. We cannot eat, sleep or work. The world has a meaning only in terms of the other person.

This is an honest, intense feeling. It is wonderful. But this one image, this restricted definition of love, also kills love. It deals with but one aspect of the process of love as if it were its only and permanent feature.

Love in our societies, in our civilizations, has been a problem leading to suicide, murder, alcoholism, sadism, torture, dishonour. Only because we want to possess. Only because we exaggerate ourselves. Only because we stoop to become so frail and vindictive. Instead of realizing our potential to become all-encompassing.

IV.

Dressed in our mental uniforms we are afraid to fully express our love. There are, for instance, gender specific ways of showing love. Deviating from these restricted categories, something that should not be considered a deviation at all but rather a liberation toward self-expression, leads to difficulties in the partner's set perceptions of each other.

Love is also expressed in such selfish, self-protecting ways that one usually dare not show one's feelings, certainly not all at once. One goes step by step, installment by installment, making sure that it is reciprocated even to the outrageous point of wanting to hear the "I love you," echo.

Our love expressions resemble the exchange system of a barter economy.

V.

We create problems for those whom we say we love because we often lie.

One of the most frequent lies by the male for instance is to say, "I love you," for the sake of momentary possession of the female body. This should not imply that there cannot be sex without love. One can be close to each other through sex in an intimate way. But it is that and no more. One need not subjugate that intimacy to the language, to the paradigm of love. The moment one does, the beauty, the spontaneity, the humanness of that shared intimacy becomes spoiled by the use of the "love lie." By being subjugated to a context in which it does not exist, cannot exist, did not exist.

How is it possible that the thought-feelings of love and hate can be experienced by the same person? How can there be an opposite of love? How can love contain the seeds of hate and hate the seeds of love?

Do they? Or is that coming from the language, a superstructure built on our thought-emotions?

Again, this has to do with the perception, function and definition of love. Hate can only come when love is looked upon as something to be consumed, as something to possess or be possessed by.

VI.

We have come to such a point in human affairs that our institutions, professions, language and even economy are based, not on the existence of love, but lack of it. Love as a problem is big business. Psychotherapists, singles bars, holiday companies, vacation villages, cruise liners, beauty institutes, fashion designers, perfume and cologne manufacturers, the advertising industry all have something to do with the search, with the yearning for love. They exist, make money, simply because falling in love, being in love, and falling out of love, can all be problematical even to the point of suffering from sleeplessness and resorting to taking sleeping pills, anti-depressants, alcohol . What a sad state of affairs for our species to have to take drugs to induce sleep, all for lack of love.

Instead of being one with ourselves and with others, we become one with the sleeping pill. Instead of reaching out to one another, instead of developing a new language of empathy, we reach out for the pill. This has become such an accepted, common practice for our species that doctors prescribe them, pharmaceutical companies make millions from manufacturing them, tens of thousands of the working class are employed in making them.

VII.

Arthur and Cynthia Koestler "went out" together. They are not the first couple to have committed joint suicide. There are many cases where one has followed the other to death. Sometimes through one's own will, sometimes by just giving up on living. An exaggerated importance has been given to both the self and the relationship by choosing death. Many death contracts are made between lovers who will kill themselves when the other dies.

Such contracts make the love relationship a prison. This is, once more, a totalitarian understanding of love.

Life is greater than love. Life encompasses love. IN LIVING we love. In loving and suffering we live. Suffering and love belong to life. Choosing only love and refusing suffering is tantamount to refusing life itself. Although we often die dramatically for lack of love, we live with and for love much less.

Anna Karenina is not a tragedy. It is a tragedy for human society that Anna Kareninas can exist.

VIII.

Our understanding of love is superficial.

The word "love" is used in relationships between parents and children, husband and wife, the individual and god, friends, our desire for hamburgers, pinocolada, gambling and fast cars. The number of contexts seems to be unlimited.

Our love feeling-thoughts have not matured.

Ancient Egyptian love poetry describes the same limited thought-feelings on love as today. Consider that Inuits have so many different words for snow and sailors for different winds. Unless ancient words for love have different meanings lost over time, we continue to express ourselves in the same unrefined, primitive and totalitarian way, as we did centuries ago.

IX.

It is a totalitarian aspect of our way of loving that we show our feelings most openly to those whom we least fear. Thus, we are least unrestrained with children and animals.

Three days ago I was walking in Marburg behind some children aged eight or nine who had apparently just come out of school. They were waving with joy at cars that passed by. Each time their waves were returned, they waved with even more exuberance at the next car. Their joy had a pleasing and welcoming effect on the drivers who waved back. I was also very happy and full of life that day. The children enhanced my exhilaration. All of a sudden I had the urge to do what they were doing. At first I couldn't. Then, I finally raised my hand and with a smile waved at the car which had just gone by the children. The passengers in the car had smiles and were waving at the children. When they saw me waving their hands dropped, their expressions changed. I continued with the next few cars until I was waving just to see if anyone would wave back — waving at the same people who had been waving to the children. No one waved back! Why?

Why can we not share our love of life with each other with something as simple as a wave?

In our sexual behaviour as well, we are restrained with our peers and completely let go with those we dominate.

A most typical example of a dominating position accompanied by unrestricted behaviour is in a brothel. What one does not express to one's partner or share with one's peers, one practices with the gayest of abandon when being able to dominate a hired slave.

X.

Totalitarian attitudes in love are mostly learned through popular songs and films.

Of those, it is the song, the love song, that has had a most determining influence. What makes the songs extremely effective is that they are short, catchy, easy to remember. Songs live for generations, sometimes being reincarnated in contemporary versions. But the messages, throughout the ages, have remained the same. "I can't live without you," "You are mine, I am yours," "Don't leave me."

"You've left me, betrayed me, ruined me."...

Throughout the ages we have repeated such songs, thereby reinforcing a particular love mindset.

"Love and marriage go together like a horse and carriage." Why?

There is no connection between the two. Yet, the connection has been imprinted in our heads to the detriment of both marriage and the horse.

The horse yet again being harnessed, this time by marriage and love, now hitched to a carriage.

Almost all love songs uphold the institutions and traditions of the established order. Love songs are an instrument in socializing us to a totalitarian concept of love.

XI.

The totalitarianism of love is further manifested in jealousy.

It should be impossible for love and jealousy to exist side by side in the same person were our concept of love not a totalitarian one. Jealousy makes no sense, unless what we mean by love is a dominating, possessing, totalitarian relationship. Jealousy is the food of long-lasting relationships says Proust. At what cost?

Another source of totalitarianism in love is from the holy books, with love being preached as the word of god.

In preaching we order. In being preached we are ordered. "Love one another," rings on hollow ears. It is an imperative sentence. The preacher is commanding us to love one another.

Never mind our neighbours and enemies, can we command our beloveds to love us? The greatest wielders of power on earth know that they cannot command love. The self-appointed preachers who have assumed a mission to spread the word have neglected those closest to them. They have neglected, ignored THE loved one.

Many preachers, missionaries have forsaken those who loved them, those whom they loved in return, only to go on with what they have claimed as their calling. I can hear them,

"No! I cannot father a child. I cannot become a mother. I must go on with my mission to sow the seeds of love in the hearts of men."

Can one love by refusing love? Can one sacrifice love for causes? Where then is love? Do we not live to love?

In preaching to others we become less.

XII.

In our practice of so-called love there is reciprocity.

I'll do this for you, you'll do this for me—a relationship of mutually fulfilling each other's needs and desires. I love you, because you love me, because I love you.

Why do we reciprocate? Because we have not found our own individual expression of love. In reciprocating we use the language of the other, setting up standards and formulas of mutually ordered behaviour. By assuming the language of the other, a common reliable construct, we do not share but submit.

Our use of language reflects that love is a formulaic give-and-take relationship rather than a shared process. "Make love to me!" "I want to make love to you!" "Love me!" "I want to kiss you!"

What demands! What imperatives! What is lacking is the word "WITH."

The moment one falls into reciprocity, the totalitarianism lurking in the wings cannot be avoided.

XIII.

The advice of psychologists in both private sessions and "self-help" best sellers is for us, i.e. their clients, to be open and be aware of the needs of one another, fits perfectly with the method and art of capitalistic discourse. Such a relationship is one in which both persons are consumers. Consuming each other. Consuming from each other.

It is the bordello, the brothel at home, where we expresses to each other our "desire demands."

In consciously pleasing the loved one we also have the power not to please. Sometimes we use this power playfully by physically teasing our partner. But is not teasing a playful reminder of the terrible power of control that we have over the other? In relationships of reciprocity, all spontaneity, improvisation are taken out of the relationship.

The brothel has come home and it's called love. The only difference is that a so-called equality has been established. Men and women, partners, make "desire demands" on each other. Perhaps, the female also being able to express her needs and desires, the expression of which had been suppressed for centuries, gives today's love relationship an aura of democracy and equality.

There is no question that in terms of biological response mechanisms, men and women are now more open to each other sexually. The exchange of sexual fantasy, free expression of desire- demands among partners is a lubricant for the body machine.

This open and honest expression means reinforcing indulgence, often at the expense of establishing strong personal bonds, that is, at the expense of love.

Thus, with the inevitable waning of physical pleasure, couples either attempt to widen the latitude of their sexual activities by trying ever new things (positions, drugs, fantasy, other persons) or leave each other to find new "love satisfaction" partners. Without suffering the great psychological shocks of yesteryear we change many love partners in one life cycle. Especially between the ages of 20-45, when the body is most biologically active. This is now a most common love paradigm. Something expected. Something normal.

Honesty in today's relationships implies a lack of responsibility.

For what is emphasized in today's love is the physical. It follows therefore that love too, now has something to do with physical fitness—a typical characteristic of totalitarian societies.

We therefore repress our very natural desire for meaningful and possibly permanent relationships. In the modern love relationship, the "till death do us part" vow is statistically a big joke (if indeed there is a marriage). It has lost its meaning by pre-nuptial contracts.

We are here for each other now. We may go our separate ways whenever the situation arises. The relationship is established by circumstance by the duration of one's stay in place of education, place of work, etc. Given that more and more of us are moving from job to job, city to city, we end up with situations in which relationships are like rented apartments and cars.

Thus, another aspect of the totalitarian love paradigm is that by repressing our desire for a meaningful, all enhancing, sharing, giving relationship we kill the potential for beauty, we kill the potential for beauty to be with each other. We kill the potential to create love.

XIV.

In our century, with the exception of traditional societies, the idea of more than one love experience is common place. More of us are falling in love more than once, and more than ever before.

The frequency of such experiences has made us more critical in our relationships. Our self-preservation instinct protects us from unrequited love. The relationship works or it doesn't. If it doesn't, then on to someone else. As quickly, and with as few complications as possible. One must preserve oneself. One must be happy. One is important. No one else is worth it.

We are taught to critically judge the nature of our "emotional investments," to make sure that we are always on top of the situation. "Don't let yourself be hurt." "You are important to yourself." "You are important!"

XV.

A further source of totalitarianism in love comes from judging one love experience in the light of another, comparing past loves and lovers with the present one on the basis of hierarchical judgments and adjectives.

This usually happens at the end of a relationship. An appreciation of the love times shared together is ignored.

In each new relationship we tell each other what was bad about the previous one. Not sharing why it did work while it did, but rather why it didn't work at the end. We judge the relationship by its end, rather than having a sense, an appreciation of the whole process.

In quantifying and categorizing love, in judging it as a loss because it ended, in judging it by its result, we cast out the love that was lived, experienced.

The comparison of love experiences is an example of trying to possess and quantify love. In quantifying we control. In trying to control we impose a totalitarian order. Love cannot be quantified. It cannot be compared. Yet, in all accounts of love, the milestones, the road markers, are the persons in the love experiences. We do not attach to the love process its own character. We do not have a sense of love but only an account of how it was with others.

When love seeks possession, we have the likes of the 18th century young Werther committing suicide over Lotte and paving the way for thousands all over Europe to do the same. When the obsession of the person, the desire to possess the other, is greater than love itself, it is no longer love. Love cannot be greater than life. Nor can it exist without freedom.

Goethe's Werther is totalitarian. There is pain in not possessing. There is imminent death in not possessing. There is a contract with the devil in an attempt to possess.

"I love you," is a totalitarian statement. It does not reflect a state of love between two persons. It cannot be given. It can only be shared. It cannot be love until it becomes a part of the shared, ever going process.

"Giving" love is also not dependent on the "acceptance" of love. Love can neither be given nor accepted. One should not have the mistaken notion that if love is accepted, then we no longer have the makings of a totalitarian situation. The 'giving-acceptance paradigm, in and of itself, has totalitarian potential. The act of acceptance, the situation of being in the position to accept or refuse, also has totalitarian implications.

Love is not something to accept or refuse. It's a state of being. It's a state of being that can only be arrived at by being in and with life—not by being on top of life, not by trying to dominate it, but by just being open to what life brings with the fullness of the self.

Love has, in and of itself, for lack of a better word, its own character.

Once the love is over and the two persons withdraw from that experience, the total, the sum, the gestalt, still remains. At the end of the relationship love is not lost. It is only two persons who have left that particular form of loving between them. But, the love between them, the love that was, has not disappeared. It is ever present. It is only because of our paradigm to look upon our love experiences through possession that we do not continue to see it. When it is over, we often look upon the love experience with bitterness, wondering why it didn't work. Blaming this and that.

The point is that it did work! For the time that we were together it did work. There was love. There will always be love.

XVI.

No work of art can take precedence over love. Love is always in the process of being created in various forms and languages—an infinity of content between two persons.

Without question, love between two persons is the most difficult of any creative endeavour. Very few of us can create love with all our senses, with all our potential available to us.

Love is a never-ending process, a continuation of all past loves in both our individual past and in our shared past as a species. Yet, something along the way has happened to love. Somewhere, sometime, within us...

Saul Bellow, "More people die of heart break than cancer."

And my father, a psychiatrist, when asked by a journalist as to what love sickness was all about, answered, "There is no such thing. Not being in love is an illness."

March 28, 1987, Marburg

TO BE DRUNK!
XX

Pan and Dionysos, Dilek Hekimoğlu, 1991

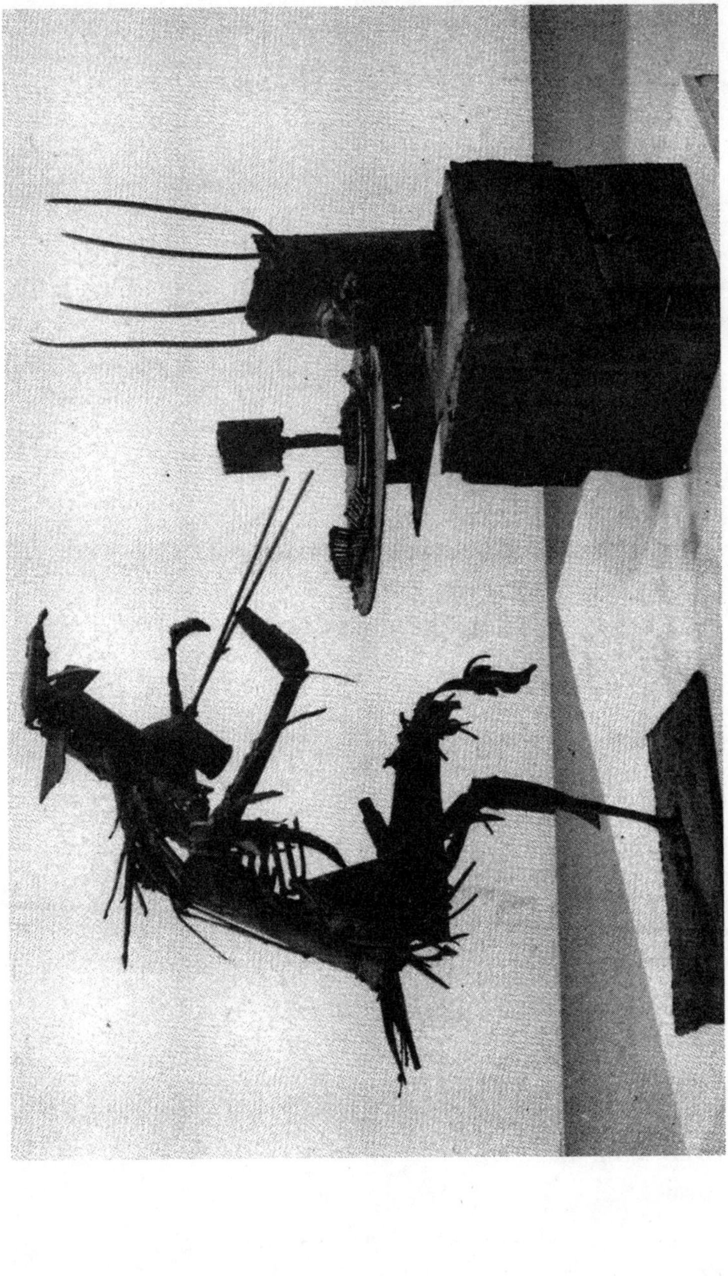

To be Drunk!

Always be drunk!
That's the question.
Not to feel time weighing down on your shoulders,
bending you down to the earth,
Be drunk!
With what?
Wine, poetry, virtue.
As you wish.
But, be drunk!
If sometime you wake again,
find yourself on the stairs of a palace,
in the green grass of a ditch,
or by yourself in the mournful solitude of your room,
No longer drunk!
Ask,
the wind,
the wave,
the star,
the bird,
the clock.

Everything that
flies,
groans,
rolls,
sings.
Everything that
speaks.

Ask them the time-
and
the wind,
wave,
star,
bird,
clock,
will answer,
It is time to be drunk!

Not to be the slaves of time,
be drunk.
Always be drunk,
on wine, poetry, virtue
As you wish...

Charles Pierre Baudelaire

(Translated from the French and
adapted from the Turkish and English by
G. Vassaf and L. Morgan)

The way out is found, Paul Klée, 1935

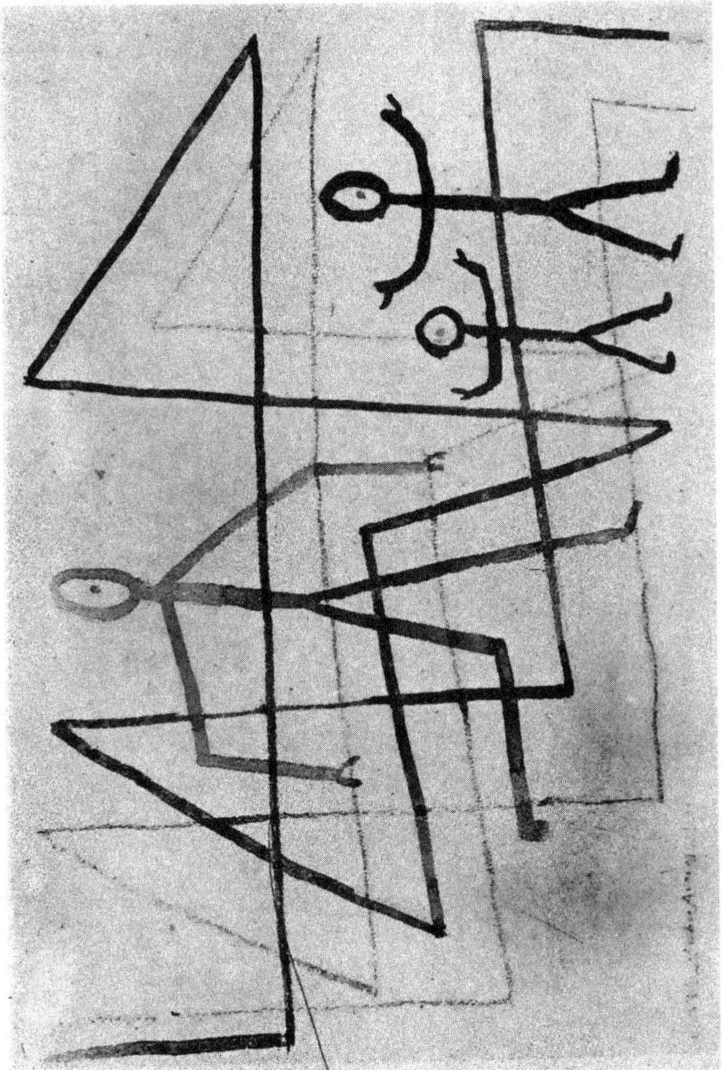